Pocket Rainbow

KAREN ESS

ISBN: **978-0-620-85033-9 (print)**
ISBN: **978-0-620-85034-6 (e-book)**
Printed in South Africa

Published by Karen Ess
Johannesburg, Gauteng 2019

Publisher's Note

This is a work of fiction based on true stories. Names changed and events muddled to protect the people involved. Any resemblance, similarity, or likeness to actual villains, living or dead, groups, business establishments, or criminal organizations is entirely coincidental.

https://kess9316.wixsite.com/kareness

DEDICATION

To the wonderful people of Alex, and especially to the orphans and vulnerable children – to your courage, and resilience, and joy. You are a great community! May you find hope and inspiration.
God bless!

Table of Contents

ACKNOWLEDGMENTS

Thank you so much to my Mom and brother, who have endured a lot of extra work whilst the book was being written. To my siblings and to all my friends for their encouragement and support. Mostly to Eurydice for her assistance with the editing. And of course to my Eternal Friend and Master, without Whom this book would never have gotten off the ground or been finished.

Preface

Karen Ess worked in the township of Alex amongst orphans and vulnerable children – child-headed households. She got to know many of their struggles and challenges first-hand, and this book is a result of her experiences.

The first two stories are based on events that actually happened, although details and locations have been changed to protect their identities. The heroes are real; the locations are real; but the villains are figments of the imagination.

The solutions, though based on true stories, are not the real solutions of the actual events, but at least the reader is drawn into the township and its issues.

The third story is pure fiction – people, events, businesses and plot are products of an overactive imagination. However, the Alex township location and houses are based on real houses, and real streets, and include all you can see, hear, smell and touch there.

I trust you will enjoy the story as much as I came to love the people of Alexandra township and its most vulnerable inhabitants.

Pocket Rainbow

Prism

The drop hung suspended from the battered gutter, for a moment catching the sun in a sparkle of shimmering colours. The girl caught her breath in a short gasp of wonder at its sheer, unutterable beauty. The pale, grey-streaked patches of wall paint, too, caught the light, and reflected the warmth and hope of the newly washed sky. Finally, the drop loosened its hold, and wended its way earthwards. She breathed a painful sigh, and trudged homeward, toes curling in the mud.

The girl passed smartly-dressed workers returning home, high heels squelching in disgust as they tried to extricate themselves from the sludge. The township was not kind when it rained. She pushed her way between two narrowly adjacent shacks, crossed the open drain, pausing only briefly as she gagged on its fetid aroma, then, flapping her way past the newly-drenched washing hanging across her pathway, she reached the dark, damp tangle of corrugated iron and cardboard she now called home. She carefully unthreaded the wire from the door - her only protection against thieves - and stepped down into her sunken, windowless cubicle. The trapped heat caught the girl squarely in the face as she moved, and the familiar smell of pap[1] and Sunlight soap[2] greeted her gently. As her bare feet touched the concrete floor, she gave them a quick, complaining wiggle, and, stooping, moved gingerly toward

---

[1] *Pap*: Afrikaans word used by black community for maize meal made into a stiff porridge that is more like soft, moist bread than gruel.

[2] Sunlight: Brand of bar of dark green soap used for hand-washing clothes. It is inexpensive, and doubles as a soap for washing the body.

the rear, where her tomato-box-seat stood proudly in one corner.

She glanced round the room, fleetingly pleased with its interior. The square-metre of green carpet-cut-off lent dignity next to the tired, musty smelling mattress her mother had retrieved from the streets. A faded brown and orange seventies-style duvet carefully covered the offending object, and performed the dual purpose of hiding most of her neatly-folded clothing that was stacked on the bed. It would not be suitable for long. She would have to find a way of raising everything off the floor because of the rats, but it would do as a start.

Her eyes travelled in the dim light from the open door to two large tins that served as pots. Shiny with scrubbing, they hung from the roof by the wire she had twisted around them for handles. Smaller tins served as cups, and an empty Omo[3] container would function adequately as a bucket for drawing water for a short time. The grass broom she had made stood tidily in a corner, having discharged its duty twice that day. No-one would have cause to call her one of those slovenly girls who were sloppy in their cleaning habits.

"The future's bright, the future's Mobi[4]", blared the radio next door. She grimaced, momentarily angry at the words. Advertisers could be so *insensitive!* What hope did *she* have now? She shook her head firmly. She wasn't going to give way to despair and anger that came so easily to her. Not now. There were more important things, such as where to find food for tonight. At least it shouldn't be too difficult. No one in Alex ever went hungry for long - people would often give to their neighbours, no matter how little they themselves had.

---

[3] Omo: Brand of washing powder
[4] Mobi: Fictional Mobile phone operator

Cyan

Truckdriver Joe Mbuti was troubled. His aunt had told him the story of the young girl who had been living in her courtyard, and who had been kicked out of home to earn her living. For three nights, he had dreamed of a girl screaming in agony. It was a long time since he had been so worried about a predicament. He was convinced he was getting some sort of message.

"It's like a splinter under the skin," he explained to his wife, "I can't get away from it. I know I'm being told to do something." Anna knew exactly what he meant by that. Like most of Alex, they shared a common faith, so she understood that he was referring to God.

He ran his hand over the back of his head distractedly. He paused. "It's so sad that young girls are on the streets," he said mournfully. "It shouldn't have to be like that. We Alex people can do something about it." He paused, frowning at the problem, "We *must* do something about it!" He shut his lips firmly and glared at his wife. "*Thuma mina.*"[5]

---

[5] *Thuma Mina*: Send me, a double reference to a song by the famous musician Hugh Masekela, and a reference to Isaiah 6:8 from the Bible. It developed into a philosophy of activism; of being the person to create change.

Anna looked up from chopping the carrots with a half-smile. What a mass of contradictions was her husband. A man who took no nonsense; a man of action, but a man of deep compassion too. He always gave money to a needy beggar, or help to an old lady to arrange her daughter's funeral. Once, he had come perilously close to giving his entire salary away to a man whose shack had burnt down. It was only her intervention that had stopped him. She inhaled, savouring the physical and emotional strength of her impetuous man.

"Well?" she murmured gently, "What must you do?"

He scowled. "That's just it!" he exclaimed, thumping the table, "I've absolutely no idea." He looked at her intently, then straightened up. Laughing suddenly, he gave her a wild kiss. "Your unpredictable husband being the hero warrior again!!"

She smiled, but quipped quickly, "Ok. But discuss with me before you go on a rescue mission." "Deal!" he replied.

Scarlet

Ntombi,[6] as the girl was called, cherished her first memory of her mother's joy. She was running down the street toward her mother. She recollected uMama's catching her up, swinging her round, and planting a delighted kiss on her chubby cheek. She remembered dancing in the shack, and skipping down the street together. They had often taken little holidays, and gone to the veld to discover insects and little flowering plants. They would take a picnic and a blanket, and stay out all day, coming home sweaty and satisfied. It seemed that the taste of happiness was never-ending.

She couldn't remember at what stage the Man had arrived. A tall stranger whom she had to call "*Baba*". Daddy. The introduction of sadness. Distance. Anger. Fights. Beatings. Their dancing had pirouetted to a halt. So had the picnics.

uMama had become very tired, and had withdrawn to the fathomless crevices of her mind where she was safe; where beauty and hope still existed. Others only saw the glazed eyes, but Ntombi knew of the force of life within.

That Sunday when the drops began drumming on the corrugated iron roof, uMama had called her into the bedroom. Her face was more sombre than usual, and looked rather pale. uMama began, "It is now time," she muttered gravely, patting the bed next to her. Her breath came in sharp wheezes: "You are 14, and a grown woman." She swallowed convulsively, as if her words were refusing to come out and were instead trying to worm their way into her stomach. "You must make your own way in the world now. You must look after yourself."

Ntombi stared at her dumbly. A torrent of thoughts whirled in her mind. What on earth did her mother mean?

---

[6] *Ntombi:* means little girl – in this case, it is a nickname

She stared at the patchy linoleum. The layers of polish looked grimy in the areas where the covering had been worn away to the concrete beneath. Years of care and attention had not been good to it.

Her mother's words came from far away. "We are too poor to feed you anymore."

Next door, the wails of children broke out, pulling at something in the room so that it seemed reality itself would snap.

Ntombi looked around the room. She glanced at the faded curtains in the window, which were swaying sombrely. Permanently closed because of the prying eyes that passed the house so closely, they darkened the room. The panes themselves were translucent and speckled with age, and their warped frames leaked cold air in the winter. Her eye scanned the unevenly plastered walls which were imbued with deep cerulean paint, and stopped for a brief moment on the nobly-suspended portrait of Nelson Mandela. Although somewhat watermarked, it had never failed to inspire her with courage. Today, it just seemed like a picture of an old man. Underneath it, the plastic faux-marquetry picture of a Japanese lake caught her eye before it was drawn to the fingers of rising damp, and speckles of mould near the door.

Suddenly, she noticed a large black plastic rubbish bag standing in a corner of the room. A lilac slipper peeped out of it. These slippers had been a gift from one of her uncles, and she treasured them greatly - looking after them with great care, and wrapping them gently in tissue paper every morning.

She also noticed a magazine sitting atop the bag. She had bought the magazine with R10 that her aunt had given her. It had been meant for food, but she had decided to splash out on a treat. She did not care that she'd had to go hungry. She wasn't going to let poverty always dictate what she could or could not buy. In that moment, she could escape, and live in a world where dreams came true....

A frown carved into her smooth brow. Why would some of her things be in the bag?

Her Mother cleared her throat uneasily. "Now, you have to make your own way in life. Find your own money for food and for rent. You know how it has been with my not finding work ..." She left the sentence unfinished.

Ntombi knew only too well. There had not been much to eat for the last few years, and with Stepdad drinking his own meagre salary away, their only new clothes were cast-offs from the local church, and their food the remains from faithful neighbours. Still, they had managed – even getting a portion of meat on Sundays - and she had believed that at least her education would offer her a way out. She had worked very hard, scarcely taking time for spending with her friends. Sacrificing much, she had spent her days at the Alex library, doing extra research, and so was doing well at school. Now it appeared that uMama no longer believed in dreams. She seemed to have given up. More than that, it seemed as though she were throwing them out and deliberately trampling on them.

uMama paused, "You can work at night, and study by day."

She stared at her mother, scarcely daring to breathe. "No Mama! No!" The whisper barely escaped her mouth. How would she survive? She only knew of one way - many girls faced the same situation. All in Alex knew that it was men who kept these girls alive. R20 a session. The price of nearly two loaves of bread. The luckier ones got a sugar-daddy.

She had always thought she would be spared the same fate. She was the one who was going to go to varsity and bring hope to the rest of the family who were so firmly captive to poverty. Now, it seemed that the dream had ended like an exploding hand-grenade, stunning her with its violence.

She had *so* been looking forward to being called by her real name - Nothemba. Hope. She'd always been called Ntombi - even at school. She hadn't minded, but her cherished wish had been to live up to her name. Now, in a heartbeat, it had been reduced to an irony. The room around her seemed to shrink, and she strained for air. She looked down at her fingers interlaced on her lap. She began clicking her thumb nails one under the other in a snapping motion. Click. Click. Click. The rhythm started to soothe her somehow. She uttered a deep sigh. *Life* was inevitable, she thought. Numbness reached her fingers and toes. Within a few more moments, her thinking, too, petered out to a blank. Reflexively, and avoiding her mother's gaze, she reached toward her black bag.

Violet

Joe had seen the girl watching the raindrop. Her joy at a such a small thing caught at his heart, and his eyes followed her as she pushed her way past some shacks. It was a pleasure to see young people enjoy what little they could of the Creation in Alex. In the distance, he saw her clamber into the small shack that everyone tended to avoid if they could. He wondered why she would stay there. It was one of the bad shacks - structurally unsound. Besides which, it was not good for young boys and girls to live without parents. All sorts of trouble awaited them when they did. He knew there were some child-headed households. Was she perhaps an orphan? He would have to ask around. He did not care to see vulnerable children preyed upon. Perhaps their community could do something, he thought. That had been on Wednesday.

He had seen her in the same spot the following day. There was a brick jutting out of the pathway, and she had bent down to remove it. Struck by her thoughtfulness, he had continued to watch as she smoothed the path. He found himself drawn to the girl's tenderness. The world needed more such people, he thought.

As he watched, she suddenly jumped up. In her hand was two R5 coins. Hidden under the brick perhaps for months, she had come upon a small treasure. He smiled at her victory dance, and turned back to his home.

Magenta

Gogo[7] Evelyn's sturdy form was sitting hunched over in thought, rather like the Rodin sculpture. The women in her Wednesday knitting circle had told her about the young girl who had been chased out of home and who was now living in one of the hidden shacks on her own street.

"*Hao!*[8] Such things should not be!" she had exclaimed. "If girls are forced to become prostitutes, it makes us look bad."

"As though we have no *ubuntu*[9]," agreed one. "What is Africa coming to if we don't help each other?"

"Ehhh!" sighed the women in chorus. They all paused a while whilst they savoured the Old Values. Many good things had happened since 1991, but some precious things were also disappearing. The continent was changing so quickly that no one could keep up.

Finally, someone spoke: "A child's entire future is being destroyed."

"We old people can't study at university" added another, "and get a good job, but the young ones ..."

"If they work very hard," agreed one woman, "they can Escape." They all understood what she meant. Poverty was the underlying statement of their every breath, and did not need to be mentioned.

Granny Evelyn was thinking about that conversation. What could *she* do? She had her own orphans to care for;

---

[7] *Gogo:* Zulu for granny
[8] *Hao*!: An exclamation of surprise
[9] *Ubuntu* - the philosophy of brotherliness that Africa has given to the world which includes sharing what you have with your neighbour.

and a *spaza*[10] shop to run. For a child of that age, a granny could not get a care-grant from the government. Her slim resources were already very stretched. Yes, she occasionally went without food - but what person would see a neighbour go hungry while she had already had a meal that day? Only a very selfish person would not share.

She grimaced, and groaned softly. Her joints did not enjoy sitting still for long. She straightened up, stretching out the discomforts. Alex could not continue like this.

She would have to speak to someone. Someone like Joe Mbuti. She would see him on Saturday.

---

[10] *Spaza* shop: tiny grocery store

Emerald

Ntombi could not believe it. Ten Rand! What could she do with it? She thought a little, and decided she would buy a large *vetkoek*[11], with lots of mince. At least she wouldn't have to beg for food this night, nor start the dreaded prostitution. She could already taste the oil-rich bread, and smell the spicy savoury meat. She could almost feel the hot juices dripping down her fingers. Her mouth watered, and her heart lifted - just a little. She tripped toward the *vetkoek* stall.

She knew she was avoiding the inevitable, but she firmly believed there *had* to be another way. She had prayed for days. She needed a miracle quickly.

---

[11] *Vetkoek:* Fried Dough

Cadmium Yellow

Joe Mbuti's mind was made up. He was convinced that the girl watching the raindrop and his aunt's girl in need were one and the same person. He was going to speak to Gogo Evelyn. This old lady was known for her practical wisdom, and ability to find things out. She would be the ideal person for advice, even if she was a bit bossy. Everyone understood she had a kind heart.

When he found her, she was in the process of closing shop. She summoned him with an imperative wave. "Joe, come and sit here for a moment."

"Hah! It's I who wish to speak to you!" he returned jovially.

"I know," she said simply. "You have something heavy on your heart."

He grinned. You couldn't hide much from this formidable woman.

"But this time I wish to ask help from *you*," she added.

He sat down on the tree stump seat outside the shop. It was going to be a long talk.

She enquired politely about his family and his work, and then exclaimed: "Now! We have serious matters to discuss."

"Indeed!" he replied. "It has been such a weight on my mind." He paused to emphasize the matter's importance. "I have not been able to sleep. I think I have heard God speaking to me." He straightened his back. "I believe He wants me to help someone. The problem is that I have not known who or how until recently."

Granny Evelyn nodded insightfully. This man was known for his firm, rapid decisions. To be uncertain would be a torment for him. "How did you find out what you were to do?" she queried with a small smile.

"I saw this young girl - probably about 14 years old, but small, and very thin."

"Malnourished?" she enquired.

"Probably," he muttered, slightly irritated at the interruption. He continued, "She had been watching a raindrop on a gutter. It was joy to see someone relish something so small." He gazed into the distance. "Beautiful!" he added with conviction. "That's what made her catch my attention."

Gogo Evelyn lifted up her head at this, and looked at him thoughtfully. "And then?" she prodded encouragingly.

"I saw her again the next day. Or rather evening. She was picking up a brick from the rough path to her shack. The unusual thing was that she removed the brick and smoothed the path over, putting the brick to the side. It seemed very much as though she was smoothing out the path...you know how often people fall on the uneven ground - especially old people. She appeared to be doing something for the community. Small, yes, and only one little problem. But not insignificant."

Gogo Evelyn was captivated. "There are such people", she mused. "Always considerate of others. We need more like her in Alex. People who *do* something. Who are kind. So many people expect the Government to do everything." She smiled ironically. "As though we are not capable of helping ourselves."

"It certainly made her all the more noticeable," Joe added. "And she was rewarded for her effort!" He beamed, and punched his arm into the air, knocking his hat off in his enthusiasm. "She found some money under that brick! Probably been there for donkey's years," he exaggerated. "No need to try find out who it belonged to."

Gogo Evelyn laughed. "Well, we won't argue about that," she said, a tinge of disappointment in her voice. "Let's just chat about why and how you want to help the girl."

Joe turned to her. "The problem is - I don't know. I need your wisdom and ideas. All of mine have other problems attached to them."

Gogo Evelyn blinked her eyes, nodded and began to discuss various options.

Sap Green

That evening, Ntombi decided to go for a walk. It was a fresh winter's evening. Small, furry bundles of cloud were strewn untidily across the sky, like children's toys in a busy nursery school. The sun was starting to set, and the heavens were a lazy blue, permeated on the horizon by the softest yellow pollution.

Smells of roasting chicken pieces mingled with wafts of garlic, onion and scorched *pap*, lingering in the air like lovers reluctant to part. An occasional drift of rotting rubbish reached her nostrils, but for once, it was the good smells that were stronger. Her shoes crunched on the sandy sidewalk, sounding like cracknel being chewed. Ntombi gave a little hop, wiggled her bum to an internal tune, and started threading her way through the crowds of people returning from work. There were always continuous streams of residents in the street from early morning until late at night, but particularly crowded at home time. Cars struggled to pass through the mass of people spilling over from the extremely narrow pavements onto the roads.

Ntombi enjoyed these times. Great entertainment was to be had on the streets of Alex. Often, it was more interesting than a soap opera. The ability to laugh at one's fellow human beings was one of the many things that poverty could not affect. Right now, there was a granny and an older man sitting on tree stumps outside a *spaza* shop. The man was gesticulating vociferously, the lady nodding her head sagely. An over energetic motion knocked his hat off, and Ntombi giggled. She paused to watch. Placing her hands behind her back, she stretched lazily against a shack wall. It was probably dusty, and some nails were jutting into her back, but she little heeded the twinges. In a way, it was comforting to face such small problems, because they helped her focus away from the bigger pain.

Rose

Joe had finished telling Granny Evelyn his thoughts that she had been abandoned or orphaned. She heaved a breathy sigh. There was no escaping this kind of story in Alex. It was everywhere. It was like the girl's situation on her street. She chewed her lip gently.

"I realise I have a long-term commitment ahead of me", Joe was saying. "It is not as if you can give a little help and it is all sorted. It takes many years to help a person." He stretched. "The girl will need so much - in more ways than money. And if she doesn't find a job after that..." his voice faded away. They both understood. Not finding a job meant one of very few things in Alex. She might land up going into prostitution anyway, or she might have a short-term boyfriend, and have a child in order to get the R250 monthly child grant - just to survive. The other option was to get a sugar daddy - a boyfriend with a job, who would provide for her until he tired of her - as long as she gratified his every whim.

"You came to me to advise you as to what kind of help you must give." Granny Evelyn nodded at the realisation. "Let me think on it a while." They sat, drinking in the sounds and smells of evening. Here and there cooking-fires were burning. The clouds were now washed with a burnt orange, in places looking as if they had caught alight. They breathed in these ancient mysteries, quietly accepting the wintery chill. Silent amongst the hustle and bustle, they watched and pondered.

Orange

Ntombi had tired of watching them. The twilight's cold fingers were curling round her limbs and ears, and she decided to walk in order to ward it off. Joe Mbuti had not seen her, or he might have called out to her. She had not eaten today, and her legs now felt a little weak; her brain fuzzy. She set off rather gingerly. The hope with which she had set out was deluding her. Or was it eluding? She couldn't think clearly. She watched the people walk past - people with good clothes, and food at home. People with hope.

Some of them were chattering happily, and calling out to one another above the music blaring on the street.

She wondered if she could be happy like that again. She thought of her mother, and how *together* they used to be. uMama coming to her when she had bad dreams. Encouraging her when work seemed too hard. The silent, shared support when the man's anger and drunkenness came. Although the chats had become fewer and fewer as her mother had withdrawn, there was still a very strong bond between them. She wondered what had caused uMama to cast her out. She could still go and see her, but....

Suddenly, the memory of the parting jabbed at her heart. She felt rejection catch at her throat like a wild dog. It tore at the latch to her emotions, opening the gate to the dam that had built up inside. Her body started shaking; her shoulders sank, her feet moved all the more slowly, she bowed her head, and started to cry - a few tears like the beginning of rain - soon a storm. She stopped, and put her arm up against a wall, leaned her head on it. She could not help that she was in the street, shaming herself. She could not cease. People were looking at her. Staring. Pointing - as she continued to pour her troubles back onto the world that had given them to her.

Anna Mbuti saw the sobbing girl. She slowed down uncertainly. No - one was going to her rescue. A stern but compassionate woman by nature, she was little able to resist such deep misery. She walked closer. "Ntombi. Little girl," she murmured in soothing tones. "What is the matter?" Ntombi didn't hear the words, but she heard some comforting sounds close by. They penetrated her heart like honey on an open wound. Slowly, she stopped weeping, and calmed to a steady hiccough. She glanced up. A kind face was hovering. "Aunty", she mumbled, instinctively polite. She took a deep breath.

"Can I help you?" The kind words almost reopened the flood gates. Her throat ached, and the corners of her mouth turned down, but she pushed her shoulders back and stood proud. "Do you have anyone to turn to for help? Anywhere to go?"

Ntombi shook her head slowly. Her heavy eyes looked blindly at the street scene.

"Come with me. We will go to Gogo Evelyn. She's always the person who can be of help."

Ntombi had heard of her, and knew she could be trusted. She hesitated, then nodded. Words would not come right now. Numbly, she allowed herself to be led back down the street. She stumbled a little, for her limbs did not want to obey her mind. They were behaving quite like toddlers still learning to walk. With the kind lady's steadying hand on her arm, she reached Gogo Evelyn's.

The same man and woman she had seen earlier were seated there. As soon as Gogo Evelyn saw them, she shuffled to her feet. "My child! Whatever is the matter?" she intoned. Without waiting for an answer, she took her hand and led her inside. The hungry look was unmistakable. "Here", she uttered indistinctly. "A bowl of hot soup, and some *pap*." Ntombi's form shook, and tears started trickling down her cheeks again, but she quickly poured the liquid into her mouth, and swallowed it before her eyes had the chance to begin leaking again. A deep breath and a few mouthfuls later, she looked up. "*Ngiyabonga kakhulu*." "Thank you very much", she whispered.

When she had finished the second bowlful, Gogo Evelyn asked, "My child, what is your name?"

"Ntombi....", she faltered. She breathed deeply, and closed her eyes briefly.

"*Nothemba!*" [12] she said decidedly.

Gogo Evelyn smiled. "A good name," she replied. "A name which does not change with circumstances," she added wisely. Nothemba smiled. This woman understood.

"You must stay here tonight." the old lady commanded.

"Yes Gogo," she answered. It would not do to disrespect such a great woman by arguing with her.

"Go and fetch your things, and when you come back, we will see about tomorrow night. And the night after that," she added firmly.

Nothemba hopped up, half curtsied, and hurried out the door. In her haste, she hardly greeted the couple in the courtyard.

"Joe, come inside," called Gogo Evelyn. "And you too Anna", she confirmed. "We have a lot to talk about, and we must do it before the child returns." They entered, and sat on the white plastic chairs set out in a stern row against the wall for guests.

"It's the girl!" Joe burst out. "The one that I've been talking about."

"Me too!" exclaimed Gogo Evelyn inaccurately. "I mean," she corrected, "that she is the girl I was going to tell you about. What a coincidence! And that she landed on my doorstep while all of us were here!!" They looked at each other in awe.

"I know what I must do," cried Joe excitedly, "I know that God would have me support the child financially. I do not have much, but children do not need too much, and I believe I must sacrifice in order to help her." He said this in a rush, as if to prevent his reluctance from speaking. He saw his wife's face, and continued, "Anna, you asked me if I had surrendered everything, and I have. You know this money was going to be a deposit on a new house. But I believe that God wants me to use some of it for this young girl." As she

---

[12] *Nothemba* means hope

continued looking at him, he added, "I'm sorry I didn't discuss this with you before...I didn't have the time."

Anna pursed her lips tightly, and moved toward the door. She stopped, shook her head, and then sighed. "I cannot argue. You are right. I will be glad to help the child." She turned around. "Though I can't say it's not hard!!" She paused. "Our house, although old, and one of the government ones, is still a good house, even if it is not ours. Alex could do with more young people being given opportunities." She turned away, then swivelled to face the others again. "I'd best go before the child gets here. I don't want her seeing me like this. With my reluctance still in my heart. She will pick up on it. Children like that are sensitive to such things."

"I will come with you." added Joe quickly. He turned to Gogo Evelyn. "I do not want her to know it's me who is paying for her upkeep", he said ungrammatically. "She may feel obligated to me, and not trust me. We can sort out where she stays another time."

"Thank you, Joe. You are a good man." It was rare to find a man so very kind, Gogo Evelyn reflected, in any part of the world. The world was full of selfish but hard-working men, or disillusioned men, or really bad men, but what the earth needed was *generous* men. "We will discuss it once we have had some sleep." She faced Anna, "You, my dear, are a very good woman. Many women would not allow their husbands to listen to their hearts, or to give sacrificially. Allow your heart to be one hundred percent in the same place as Joe's."

Anna smiled, and put her hand on the door. "Night, Gogo," she said.

"Night *bazalwane*[13]," she returned.

---

[13] *Bazalwane* means brethren.

Cobalt Blue

After they had left, Gogo Evelyn set about clearing a space for the girl to sleep. The 6 children she looked after were at soccer and netball until 6.30 pm, so she had a little time on her hands. Nothemba could share the mattress of the oldest orphans who were 10 years old. That would be ample space for them all. She knew there were people who slept one to a mattress in the suburbs, but that was very uncharitable when there were so many people without beds. Besides which, how did they keep warm in winter?

Her thoughts turned to the girl. This girl was in serious trouble, and she might have rescued her at the critical moment. Gogo Evelyn could see she hadn't yet had to go the way of the girls of the street. It harmed a girl of her type more than others.

Did she know of any other person that she could trust to nurture this delicate girl?

The boys came bursting in at the door, so she busied herself with their meal and homework preparation for the morrow. The girls arrived at the same time as Nothemba, so she introduced them and had the latter wash the dishes whilst she settled the children for the night.

Finally, she sat down with a cup of hot tea, and invited Nothemba to sit at her feet.

"I want to know your story," she enquired gently. "Some ladies on the street have told me a little about your predicament, but I think it best to hear it from your own lips." Haltingly, and with a few long pauses, Nothemba told her story. Gogo Evelyn listened without speaking. Now and then she reached out and patted the girl on the shoulder, or laid it gently on her head for a moment. She nodded. "It's worse than I thought," she said. "It will be very difficult for us to support you if your parents are still alive." She caught her breath. "It would bring such shame on them if we supported you and took you in." With a tear in her eye, she muttered, "Why does it have to be so complicated?"

They sat in silence for some time. Finally, Gogo Evelyn got to her feet. "Well!", she announced, "We are your family too! If your aunts and uncles can't or won't take you in decently, then we will look after you. It will be tricky, but we'll find a way to satisfy that stepfather of yours. And your mother. You just can't go home to that angry man. He will take any money we give you. So, that's settled then. You will stay here!" she confirmed. "I am the only person strong enough to confront those people, if they cause trouble."

Nothemba smiled - uncertainly at first, then she jumped up and wrapped her arms round the old lady and gave her a firm squeeze. "Thank you!" she said, in a watery voice. "I am so thankful. To God. To you. To anyone else." She stopped, and added jerkily, "I am so glad I didn't have to ...."

"No need to say it," commented Gogo Evelyn. "It's over now."

The girl sighed, and looked at her with seriousness. "Yes, but I am just one. There are many out there who are like me. What can we do about them?"

Gogo Evelyn put her arm round Nothemba's shoulders. "One day at a time, my dear. One person at a time." She smiled, and they turned and walked out the room.

The colour of justice

Gladys

The reality of the morning snaked slowly into her consciousness, its whispering tendrils pulling at her eyelids, and releasing them with a flutter. Some sunlight had escaped inside through a slit in the curtains, and seemed to illuminate that subterranean feeling of horror, waking her starkly. Unreality whirled around her like a tornado. It was still there - that sense of being in the world of the Matrix. She tried to steady her head with her hand. It could not have happened. It simply wasn't possible.

Ok, she'd got pregnant, like most of the other girls in Alex. She was very popular with the guys. Of course she would be. She was wild. And pretty. With no Mom, and an older sister to look after her who didn't care and wasn't there, it was kind of inevitable. Boys always had the potential to provide an escape. The promise of being cherished and looked after - even by a poor schoolboy instead of a working man - was too rich to turn down. And the alcohol and dagga…well, it all went with the territory. Besides, a baby brought the promise of love. Of someone to belong to. Of significance and purpose.

So, the pregnancy. Schoolteachers weren't amused that she was one of the 80% of their girls who got pregnant during their school career, but it wasn't their life. Gladys sighed. She had passed her grade 11 well anyway. She knew how bright she was compared to the other kids. But then The Thing Had Happened.

The bed groaned under her as she stumbled to her feet. The familiar fragrance of her sister's burnt *pap*[14] touched her nostrils. Stretching gingerly, she eased the sleep out of her shoulders. She frowned as she caught sight of a bump on her arm. Mosquitoes seemed unusually tenacious this year. They

---

[14] *Pap* is corn porridge

were always plentiful in the summer, but they burnt those candles with stuff in them. The whatyoumacallit. Citronella. It almost seemed to draw them instead. Her unwashed odour drifted to her attention. Ugh! Time for a wash! Her foot jerked up as it touched the cold concrete floor, and her body shivered in disapproval. Uncaringly, she pattered slowly to the bathroom. They had running water, so they could fill the tin tub, but the water still had to be heated on the stove. She wasn't going to bother. Cold water might help to clear the mouse nests in her head.

They all lived in a 2 bedroomed unpainted RDP[15] house. Five of them. Two girls and three boys. And occasionally her sister's boyfriend. Definitely better than a shack. It even had a *butler*[16], or *stop-nonsense* on the front door.

"Glaaaaad!" came her sister's cross voice.

"What Now!" she whispered, too tired for an argument.

"Glad!" The short, sharp bark irritated her.

"No!" she yelled back rapidly. "Just shut up!" She sniffed. "And it's not Glad. It's Gladys." (At least it was better than "Badglad," which was a favourite punishment tag.)

Her sister's scowl popped out of the bedroom door. "What did you do with my comb?" she asked accusingly.

"Xh!" Clicking in her tongue in exasperation, Gladys snarled, "I fed it to the rats. What did you think?" She glared at Irene. "You always blame me - but you constantly forget where you put things. Whydon'tyoulookunderyourrug? You'llprobablyfindyouhiditundertheresoIcan'tgetatit," she uttered speedily, but Irene had disappeared with a doorbang. "Arrgh!" she screeched in exasperation, then did an about face. "Oh!" Gladys whispered to herself, "What's wrong with me this morning? I'm so awful! My sister may be a hag, but that doesn't mean I have to be one! Crotchety, *crotchety* ugly old me! Why can't I be kind and sweet tempered?" Hunched over in discouragement, she switched on the tap for her icy wash.

---

[15] RDP: Reconstruction and Development programme aimed at redressing wrongs of apartheid.

[16] *Butler*: English word readapted to mean security gate. Also called a 'stop-nonsense' by people of the township.

Nomkhize

Nomkhize was still on the tablets. A mist had entered her mind that night, and she was still swirling in the dark three months later. It was a darkness as deep as the gold mines her dad had worked in. They had put her in an institution to try and cure it, but there had not been much change. She turned in bed. The mattress felt cold from her sweat, despite the warmth outside, and the grey-white walls seemed as welcoming as the dripping tap beating its prison tattoo. A sleepless night, with its vivid nightmares, added to her misery, and she was in no frame of mind to face the world. It was a recurring dream, where she woke with a dark face tormenting her; accusing her of being a killer. The police had said that they had no way of knowing which one of them had done it, but it must have been her. She had been the closest.

"Murderess", shrieked the demons in her dream.

"Monster!" shouted the faces of the nurses as they gave her medicine.

"Traitor!" "Vile, creepy, worthless Thing!"

She sat up, shoulders hunched and eyelids drooping. "Aaah!" she moaned. Tears rained down on her crumpled sheet, as she sucked at the air for sobbing breaths.

"Ai, *Ntombi* ," came a voice, "Not again." Gently, it continued, "Get up now." As the person belonging to the voice spoke, she wrapped a blanket around the girl's shoulders, patted and tidied the pillows; and straightened the sheets. "Remember what we discussed?" she whispered.

Nomkhize sniffed, and screwed up her nose. "Yes, Nurse", she quavered. "Get up, get dressed, eat and go to exercise, no matter how I feel.'

"And focus on positive thoughts. "

"Hhh", she sighed. "Ok." She gave a smile that made her look even sadder.

"Come on," the nurse teased. "That was a baboon smile."

Nomkhize gave a little choke.

"Ah now, that was better. Let's get up and go. Remember not to think of what happened. Only in therapy."

"It's the dreams" she burst out.

Nurse looked at her in surprise. "That's the first time you've mentioned dreams...?" Her voice ended in a question mark.

"I know. I couldn't talk about them before... but now... Now I can't cope with them anymore."

Nurse pursed her lips. "Lovey, I think we need to see that you get breakfast first. Then we'll sit down and talk. Hmm?" Nomkhize gave a half nod.

Hope

Gladys was shivering. Her legs were sticking to the plastic chair on which she was seated whilst watching what could be seen of the TV. The snowy picture and distorted sound remained the central focus of most households in Alex. It was never off, except if they were out. "Like a little god", thought Gladys - "always there - in every conversation; its noise even accompanying sleep and bathing."

Her thoughts turned to the day ahead. Her social worker was coming in this morning. Carey. Gladys couldn't stand her. She was intrusive and asked annoying questions all the time. All she wanted to do was pump as much information out of her as she could. She didn't share anything about her own life. That was so rude! Really, some white people didn't know how to behave, she thought crossly, and then corrected herself. Okay, perhaps just this one. She was supposed to help, but she just kept bumbling. She really hadn't a clue what she was talking about. Gladys got so irritated with her that she told her untrue stories about herself - she didn't want the social worker to know the truth - she would make a complete mess!! It was strange how her arrogance blinded her to the fact that she just had no people skills.

"Ugh," she grumbled out loud. "I need to make a complaint about her. I want another counsellor."

She shifted her weight, ungluing her legs from the chair. "Ouch!", she yelped angrily. "Why can't we have Normal Chairs? I can't *stand* these. "Her daily headache had commenced, her clothes smelt musty, and she had not had enough to eat.

"Make some more *pap* then!" her sister had replied when she complained she was still hungry. Gladys had stormed to the sink, thrown her plate in, and marched out the house. An hour later, when her sister had gone to work, she returned to get ready for school. Watching TV delayed her, so she was late. Scuffing her shoes, she marched to school in the rising heat. She had forgotten about the social worker.

The day did not improve at school either. Apart from detention for tardiness, she had cheeked the teachers, slapped a classmate on the face, and kicked a chairleg off a chair in frustration. The extra punishment for her behaviour only added to her annoyance. Why did no one understand? Her suffering was enough. She did not want to take more - they should just leave her alone if she was naughty.

Thinking about it on the way home, she flipped a stone with her shoe, and tripped, twisting her ankle a little. "Ei*na!*" [17] she yelled. She leant her hand on a waist high wall and rubbed at her leg. "Pshew! Today is not a good day." She gave a grunt of exasperation and swore.

"Hao ntombi!" exclaimed a soft voice near her.

Oh Lord! Not one of those preachy grannies. "Today of all days," she muttered.

"Is something the matter? Can I help you?"

The questions came so gently that Gladys' breath caught. Her eyes smarted, but she answered inaudibly, "Go away old lady."

A hand was placed softly on her shoulder, and she felt strangely quietened. With narrowed eyes, she examined the old lady: short, frail and thin, yet with a radiant light in her face. Kindness seemed to be knit into every wrinkle. Gladys felt oddly comfortable with her. She allowed herself to relax slightly.

"Look at me!" the little voice insisted.

Gladys glanced at her, puzzled.

"How long have you been carrying this pain?"

This Granny could see into her soul. It was definitely uncanny. She wriggled her body against the weight of her satchel.

"You are carrying it alone." came the voice. "That is not good."

Was the Granny one of those shaman women? A *Sangoma*?

"Do you read books?"

---

[17] *Eina* = ouch. An exclamation of pain.

She wrinkled her face at the lady in confusion. "Yes, *Gogo*." She surprised herself with her politeness.

"Ah, that is good. Me, I cannot read books," was the reply, "but I can read people." She scrutinised the young girl. "It's easy when you know how."

Gladys looked longingly at the lady. She didn't know why, but she wished to stay, and drink in all that the lady had to offer, but all she spat out was, "What do you *want*?" She felt irked by the lady's responsive smile, but curious enough to wait for the slow reply.

"No, no. I think it's what *you* want that's important." This was said with such gentleness that Gladys could not possible misinterpret a sting in the words.

For once, she had no retort. An unfamiliar fluttering of hope trembled about her waist. "*Gogo*...," she started. "I..." Once again, her own words astonished her. "I want to talk to you," she blurted out.

"Very well child. Wait while I finish sweeping the yard."

Gladys sat on the wall, and watched the lady wielding her broom with a cheerfulness that could not be disguised. Now and then she had to stop to place her hand on her back, but the discomfort seemed only to spur her on. It was a cheerful yard - some bright yellow flowers had managed to grow in the corner, and were surrounded by a small patch of prim and proper grass. The rest was cemented - but clean, and somehow inviting. The windows of the house were ornamented with beautiful blue curtains, swept back to welcome the sunshine in; and the back door glowed with polish. Two dark green plastic chairs were standing outside, adorned with faded light green cushions. They were rather limp, and the holes in the cushions had been carefully stitched, but they carried an air of elegance and welcome.

When the last particles of sand and crispy, freshly thrown litter had been swept out into the road, Gogo Miriam beckoned and smiled. It was a beam that caused her eyes to disappear in folds of skin. She turned to the house, brought the chairs forward, and placed them so that they were both angled toward the street. "Now then. You can sit so you don't have to look at me," she said. They settled themselves comfortably.

"Sometimes, it's hard to begin, so I'll start. I have had a very hard life, "She paused at Gladys' look of surprise. "Oh yes. More tough than most people in Alex."

Gladys stared at her. It was very hard to believe.

"Many people know me as Gogo Miriam."

Ah, thought Gladys, this woman was legendary for the struggles she had been through.

"Hmm. I see you know", murmured Gogo.

"But you're so happy,"

Gogo Miriam smiled. "I think," she replied, "that *that's* a story for another day. It's your turn now. Tell me *your* problems." She added simply, "I give good advice."

The Dreams

Nomkhize was seated on the grass with Nurse Jacobs. They were looking through the brokenness of the boundary fence at the township busyness. School was just out, and the cars, taxis and children vied for space on the busy streets. Screams, shouts, and hooting competed with sanity for chieftainship.

In the yard, the grass was overgrown and patchy; and the yard scattered with litter from outside, but it was pleasant compared with the interior. Here, the sky was a faded blue, and the sun fierce, scorching sections of her dress as she sat in the shade of a spindly thorn tree. She would gladly welcome the orb's heat if it would melt her to oblivion, but as she knew that would not happen, she was grateful for the shelter.

The fetid stench from the drains was stronger today. She could even taste it. Perhaps it was all part of her punishment. She opened her nostrils and inhaled deeply.

"Tell me now - those dreams of yours. Do you always have them?" Nurse's voice interrupted her self-absorption.

"Yes", her voice came wanly. "Every night. The same type of dream. "Just different faces."

"What do they look like?" broke in the nurse.

She frowned. It felt like she had been slapped. "Slowly! I want to speak slowly. And please not so loud!" She drew in some air, and adjusted her weight to another point of contact with the ground. "They look terrible. Like demons. Well, who knows what *they* look like, but I couldn't think of anything worse." She swallowed, and fixed her gaze on the horizon for a few moments. Still staring, she continued, "Black, green distorted faces. Faces with horrid expressions...sneering; jeering; angry. They frighten me terribly. Worse than anything I've seen on TV." Again she paused, opening and closing her mouth as if mechanically trying to force the words out.

Nurse Jacobs looked at her, silent in her understanding. Even if she had not been paid for doing it, she would have listened with her heart. She knew she had to work hard at curbing her natural garrulity, but years of practice had made it easier. Silence was so often a kind of caring.

"I..." Nomkhize's eyes watered. Her voice strained to conquer the tears... "They tell me I am a murderess! Over and over. I know I am. What can I do? I can't take it back!" she shrieked the words out to the world.

Overhead, a Hadida Ibis took fright, and flew onto the roof of the building, screaming its noisy protest. "I killed the baby. I must have. None of us knew who had done it. We were all too drunk....it was only 5 days old." She sobbed. "Five days."

"I was only fifteen. And already a murderess."

"How did it happen?" queried Nurse softly.

With a rush, Nomkhize continued: "We were celebrating the birth of Gladys' baby." She sniffed. "When we were too tired, we all slept on the bed. We woke up in the morning and the baby was dead. We tried and tried to breathe life into it, but we couldn't.

We couldn't imagine how it could be possible. We ran to the neighbour's house with the baby and called the ambulance, but they could do nothing."

She broke down, placing her head in her hands, and curling her legs up to her face. "Nothing." she cried. "Absolutely zero." Her weeping deepened, and she rocked her body back and forth. Then she turned to lie prone on the ground, and beat it with her fists, thin legs kicking helplessly.

Nurse waited, now and again placing a hand briefly on her shoulder. "Ok," she whispered. "OK." She knew about it, of course. The police report stated that the baby had been suffocated - one of them might have slept on the little girl, and stopped her breathing. It might also simply have been cot-death. It was not possible to tell.

None of them could remember, nor did any of them have mothers to tell them how to look after a baby, so they would not have known not to do that. The police were reluctant to spend the money on forensic analysis of the fibres in the baby's nose, because it would be too expensive...and unnecessary. Mothers sometimes slept too close to their babies - it was a known fact; it was never on purpose, and there were far more serious crimes to deal with. So the girls were left in a state of unknowing.

"The nurses all look at me with the same face as the demons. They all hate me for being a murderess." The little voice could hardly be heard, muffled as it was by the ground, but Nurse took a firm line at imagined negativity. She waited while the girl sat up and straightened her dress. After wiping her nose with her arm, she touched her fingers to her tears, rubbing them into her skin. Collecting her breath, she nodded.

"Brave girl," uttered Nurse. "You have to know," she continued, "that we do not think you are a murderer." She looked directly at the girl. "It was an accident, and no one meant to kill anyone. We feel deeply for you - anyone of us could have done the same. We do not judge you, or condemn you, so please don't insult us by thinking that we accuse you. Your mind is making that up." She waited for the words to sink in. "I know that for a certainty."

Hope quivered in Nomkhize's eyes. She examined Nurse's face, searching for truthfulness. She popped a sigh from her lips. "Thank you." She waited while processing her thoughts. "I think....perhaps...you could be right."

"What concerns me is that up till now you have not spoken of these thoughts. Or of the incident. I think something can be done about the nightmares with medication..." she stopped at Nomkhize's look of dismay. "It's ok - it won't make you feel groggy. But I think we must talk more often about these things. It is healthy."

Nomkhize nodded. "I think I want to rest now. I feel very tired."

Nurse stood up. "Yes. Let's go and talk to the doctor to get something to make you sleep well. Then, tomorrow, we can start again."

Nomkhize grabbed Nurse Jacob's proffered hand and pulled herself up. Something had shifted inside, like a gear, and she felt a release of pressure. Small, it is true, but noticeable. For the first time in weeks, she stood up straight, and lifted her head. Then she started walking back with Nurse Jacobs toward the building.

Gogo Miriam

Gladys had just finished telling Gogo Miriam the story. "My dear!" exclaimed the old lady. "What a terrible experience! Oh you poor girl." She had been holding the girl's hands in her bony ones, and she now rubbed them warmly. "You must feel so deeply about it. My child, I know all about guilt. And shame."

She shook her head in remembrance. "What about the other girl?" she asked suddenly. "Thandeka?" Gladys looked at her with a wry expression.

"You've told me about Nomkhize and yourself. But what about the other girl?"

"Huh!" she snorted, "she doesn't care. She has just carried on with her life as normal. No sadness. She was the only one who had not handled the baby. She was not really interested in children. Then she said that such things happen, and walked out of my life. She has become very harsh. She's always been a party girl, and it's no different now. But she has changed." She frowned in concentration. "Mostly her eyes have changed."

"Eyes?" queried Gogo Miriam.

"Yes, they are hard. No feeling or care in them. Just hatred."

"Perhaps, deep down..." began Gogo Miriam.

"No!" interrupted Gladys. "She is really unaffected by this."

"I think," said the granny, looking at her shrewdly, "It's best not to talk about her much...Did you suspect who *did* accidentally lie on your baby?"

"No. We couldn't work that out. Nomkhize was lying closest to the baby when we woke up, but that doesn't mean anything. We did start arguing about it, but it kinda stopped when Thandeka left to clean the baby vomit off her breast pocket." She stopped a moment, puzzled. Her eyes widened. "I thought..." She left the sentence unfinished.

"Yes?" interrogated the granny.

"Nothing!" she finished. "I think I'd best go now."

"Come again," invited Gogo Miriam. "I think that next time I will talk, and I will show you how to find forgiveness."

Gladys looked at the tiny lady, mouth frozen open. Eventually she answered, "I will come." She paused to make a rapid decision. "Tomorrow."

Thandeka

She knew. That stupid baby. How could she have kept it anyway? Didn't people give such things up for adoption? It had spoilt their fun. Although they could still have some men. And drink. There was nothing else.

She lay on her back, looking around at her shack. It had been raining, so it smelt musty. Of course, the leaking would never stop, because it was built over a stream. She was the one who had to sleep on the floor, trying to miss the water. There was no mattress - only pieces of cardboard.

Thandeka swore, and turned over. Shards of sunlight had penetrated the hut, piercing like razorblade. They lit up a shirt hung over a chair. The vomit on its pocket. It would not wash out. That idiot of a girl thought it was herself. But Thandeka knew. It wasn't human anyway. Just a moving, wailing, moaning pooh-bucket. A vague memory of lying on something warm and soft. Of wriggling. Of being unwilling to move quickly. She knew. And wasn't bothered.

She would wear that ring today. The big, multicoloured one. It had been made for her by a jeweller boyfriend, and was very distinctive. It always made her feel happy.

Justice

Gladys was walking to Gogo Miriam's. The day had gone swiftly, without calamity. She had not even had a headache. It felt a little too good. Ahead, the road was closed. It looked like a red funeral- tent18 that stretched across the entire width of the road. "Every week." she thought. "So many people dying." It was a little unusual on a weekday, but some preferred it that way. As she neared the scene, she saw that what she had thought was a tent was in fact a Coke truck lying on its side. Five police cars and an ambulance accompanied the broken glass and curious bystanders. Cola had sprayed all over the road, and was still puddling in places. Just as Gladys reached the accident, the ambulance pulled away.

"Terrible tragedy," gossiped one man. "That driver must be angry with himself."

"Who will tell the family?" queried another mournfully.

"It will all depend on if they find out who she is...It will take them hours to find something to lift that trailer."

"What happened?" asked Gladys curiously.

"Well, this truck was trying to pass a car parked on the opposite side of the road without scraping it. The driver must have been new to Alex, or he would have known - the embankment on that side is more steep than you think. Of course, the wheels lifted too high on that side and the truck fell over."

"Sorry for the girl trapped underneath," breathed another.

---

18 In Alexandra, people place a tent in the street outside the house for holding guests and refreshments after the funeral. Their yards are too small to host many people; and the streets too narrow to hold more than the tent. Thus, that street remains closed to through traffic.

"What....?" puzzled Gladys. She could not work out who they were talking about. "Oh!" she gasped. A grey hand was poking out from underneath the tarpaulin. She had thought it was a dead rat. She felt sick, and moved to sit in a glassless spot before she fainted. As she did so, the sun caught something on the limb, and it glinted. Curious, she stopped and squinted at it. Suddenly, she drew in her breath sharply. The ring! No one else had a ring like this in the whole of Alex. The multicoloured jewel seemed as though it was dancing in the light - for all the world looking like it was celebrating. Galvanised, she leapt past the policemen, and knelt beside the rubbery appendage. Gently touching the ring, she whispered, "Thandeka!" Her voice cracked. "No!" A tear welled up in her eye, and trickled slowly down her cheek. "No!"

"Ntombazan'!"[19] commanded a loud voice, "move away from there please. Don't touch anything." The policeman moved over to Gladys. "She's gone now. There is nothing you can do. "

Firm hands lifted her onto her feet, and drew her to one side. "Red," she murmured dazedly. "Guilt."

"What's that?" requested the policeman.

"Red... it's the colour of guilt," she repeated.

"Ntombazana," he said, "you don't have to worry. It's not your fault."

"No, no!" she cried. "It's not that."

"Well don't you worry. Red is not the colour of guilt. Where I come from it's the colour of justice." he remarked. Gladys looked up at him. "Justice," she repeated slowly, and then laughed a little hysterically. "Justice."

She turned and walked toward the Gogo. Slowly. Life was *just*, after all. Still, justice did not feel that satisfying in the end. Instead, it felt empty.

---

[19] Ntombazana: young girl

Mud in my shoe

With a nod to Agatha Christie's Tommy and Tuppence, two of my favourite literary characters, as well as several of the teens from the child-headed households, who may recognise their own homes here.

The Stranger

Themba Gumede lay cramped under the slanted corrugated iron sheets. The ground beneath was cold, hard and wet, and the smell of rat was overpowering. The noise of his heart thudding in his chest echoed round the little hiding space. He hoped his shoes were not sticking out.

The rough-edged voices grew closer in the uncannily quiet night.

"*Xh!*"[20] The speaker exclaimed, "No one here! I told you you'd imagined someone."

"Mmm," murmured another, deep voice. "Not convinced."

A muffled shout from down the road roused them from their speculations. "Run!" uttered the first speaker, "they found something."

A rapid patter of footsteps followed this utterance, but Themba felt another presence. Staying motionless, he held his breath. That would calm his noisy heartbeat. After a few moments, the echo resided, and he heard the man breathing a few steps away. The latter shuffled around, moved a few pieces of scrap, and finally moved away.

Themba breathed a quiet sigh of relief and moved his right foot slightly to ease the pins and needles coursing freely through his limb. He dared not exit his hidey-hole until he was absolutely sure no one was waiting silently outside.

---

[20] *Xh* – loud inhaling click, derived from the Nguni languages. Expresses disgust or irritation.

Thankfully, there had been no feral dogs to broadcast his whereabouts. They wandered all over the township, flea-infested and disease-ridden, mangy, ribs showing through their thin coats. They were a menace, but generally tolerated. Tonight, they would have caused his death.

After twenty minutes of listening for any movement, he was satisfied he was safe. It had been a fraught half-hour prior to that. He'd been ambling along through a skinny alley between the shacks of Alexander township when he had narrowly missed being caught up in a shootout. He'd seen the glint of the gun in the moonlight a split second before he would have exited the shadows. Two or three loud booms had breached the silence, and he had rapidly scuttled away, but not before he had seen the shooter's face.

He had heard stumbling footsteps behind him, and then several quiet screams of pain before he had managed to hide himself. The footsteps had had passed by his hiding place, and then then he had lain quiet as other footsteps thumped closer. Gun-carriers were not people to mess with.

After the last of the men had gone, he eased himself painfully out of the hidey-hole. No-one was about, so he dashed between some shacks to ensure no one had given chase. Slowing down after a few twists and turns, he suddenly stopped short at a loud groan. He looked searchingly into the darkness, but couldn't see anything.

A second groan, louder than the first, enabled him to zone in on the source. A man lay behind a sheet of wood, *tekkie*[21] sticking out like a flag. His arm lay strangely twisted around his chest, and he was lying in a dark puddle. His eyes looked blearily up at Themba, his face a perfect reflection of the moon.

"Er...gumph..."

Themba leaned closer.

"Hide me!"

It didn't take long for Themba to make up his mind. A man in danger of losing his life, no matter his occupation,

---

[21] *Tekkie* South African for trainer, sneaker

came first in his book any day. Besides, he had not like the look of those men.

Moving rapidly, he bent down to put his arm under the man's shoulders. Slowly, and with not a few rests, he hoisted the man to his feet. A warm sensation on his forearm alerted him to the blood.

"Ugh," he muttered, and tried to ease the man off his arm in order to find the bleed.

"Shelter!" urged the man. "First. Quickly!"

Responding to the desperation in the man's voice, Themba, half carrying the stocky man, moved through the maze of shacks toward 12th Avenue, where he lived. The man gave a few agonized cries, but simply urged Themba to move faster.

It still took them half an hour to reach the large brick room which served as a home. Themba's brother Moses was sleeping – his snores could be heard twov doors away. The curtain dividing the cooking from the sleeping area was drawn, and Themba drew it aside. He placed the man on a chair while he laid a pile of cardboard and newspaper on his mattress, then eased the man on top. The bleeding seemed to have stopped, but Themba tore a clean, old t-shirt into long, wide strips, and tied it around the man's chest.

The man was near to fainting, but managed to mouth the words, "The brooch! Find it! The blood...cover the place where I was hiding," before sinking back onto the mattress.

Themba hesitated, looking over at his older brother, but decided against attempting to wake him. Moses was notorious for the depth of his sleeping. Probably nothing on earth had the power to wake him, Themba thought. Not even an earthquake.

He nodded to the man, grabbed his torch, and rushed out the metal door, not forgetting to lock the butler[22] behind him.

The two boys had lived on their own since their parents had died, one after the other, of the Disease That Must Not Be Mentioned. Moses had been sixteen, Themba twelve, and

---

[22] *Butler, or stop-nonsense* is the term for security door in Alex

they had managed to survive since then – Themba wasn't quite sure how. However, he was not going to jeopardise their home to any more danger by any small action – such as leaving the butler undone.

Gathering up some sand in his pockets, he set out to search for drops of blood on their path to the house, scattering the sand on top of anything that looked like it might be blood. It was a little difficult in the moonlight, so he was rather generous with the sand, but that was significantly better than having some *tsotsis*[23] arriving at his doorstep with guns. Shoot first, ask question later, was the motto of such people. He began to search more rigorously.

Every now and then, he had to stop to allow cat-sized rats to pass by. They, too, were the scourge of Alex, and wandered around viciously, sidling into homes, biting children, and feeding off the piles of rotting rubbish in the road. Alex was a haven for all sorts of rats, he mused. Even the criminal kind.

---

[23] *Tsotsis*: Gangsters

A Scrap of Paper

He finally arrived at the site where the man had lain. Quite a mound of sand was needed to cover the blood there, but he worked swiftly and thoroughly. In doing so, he noticed something shining in the moonlight, stuck into a torn piece of paper. He stooped down, wondering if they were connected to the mysterious man.

He picked them up off the ground and examined them in the torchlight. A torn piece of paper, with the words, "*trouvela en casa de guerrero NM – jardin - bajo pimien....Thurs 21, 7pm.*" printed crudely in pink. What sort of language was that, he wondered?

And then there was a sparkly brooch-pin. He popped both in his pocket for later examination, and turned to walk back.

What he saw caused his heart to perform several gymnastic contortions. To the side, moving slowly, was small knot of muscular men – built along the lines of Arnold Schwarzenegger, but with a sense of menace in their body language. They did not seem to have seen him yet, for they were looking ferociously at the ground. Slowly, so as not to draw their eyes and suspicion to himself, he sidled into a nearby passageway, and hurtled into the rabbit warren he knew so well. Only after he twisted and turned through many alleyways did he stop.

He was out of breath - but not from running. His heart was now pounding loudly in his ears, and his reddened face was dripping with fear. He took a few deep breaths, and began to pick his way across the township roads to go back home. A police car passed him, crawling in the direction from which he had come. Once it had gone, his stomach settled back into its accustomed place, and the cogs of his brain chugged back into gear. He did not want to know what had happened back there, but at least he was out of it. He breathed a sigh of relief, and squatted on the ground to examine his find.

The paper was somewhat crumpled and dirt-smudged, but it was very expensive. It was thick, and showed a definite weave. He had never seen paper like it. It also smelt of something. Some sort of flower? He would have to ask Elizabeth. She knew all about aromas.

"It was the brooch that fascinates me the most," he relayed a little later the next morning at her house. Both the man and Moses were still sleeping, and he felt comfortable enough to leave them be for half an hour. He didn't think the man would wake for a long time.

"It seems to be made of gold, or gold-plating."

They gazed at it together.

"Do you know the difference between gold and gold-plating?" Elizabeth Khosa, his best friend and confidante from babyhood, shot the question at him excitedly. "And do you think the brooch belonged to the fallen man?"

"No. I don't think so," he responded waveringly to her second question. He tended to ignore some of her questions, as he got a bit confused by her cross-examination.

"How do you know?" she countered. "It could be."

"Well, what were those *skelms*[24] looking for then? They were searching very carefully for something." He wrinkled his forehead. "And a brooch is not worn by a man."

"But," she interjected with a grin, "they could just be checking for clues as to where he went."

"Sure," he admitted slowly, "we'll just have to ask the guy. If he wakes up."

"Ok, let's have a look at that brooch. "

They placed it on the table and peered at it carefully. It formed a swirling curve, much like a wave. On top of it was a flower – made of red jewels or false jewels. That it all formed a symbol was obvious – but of what?

"It certainly is strange," mused Elizabeth. She paused, and then added, "Well, it looks like we have a mystery on our hands!"

---

[24] *Skelms*: thugs

"Let's be detectives, and solve the mystery!" she exclaimed happily.

Themba looked at her sceptically – Elizabeth had wild ideas sometimes, and he was always tumbling into trouble because of it.

"Do you know how dangerous those guys are? They could harm us terribly."

"Nonsense!" she countered his qualms. "They don't even know who we are. They don't know where that man is. We are in absolutely no danger."

"But if we start asking questions, they are bound to find out. Someone is bound to tell them."

"Then we'll just have to be careful, and ask people we trust," she parried.

He just gazed at her. He knew he was already defeated. He had never been able to out-argue her. They had been friends all their lives, and her vibrancy won him over nearly every time. He knew he would not be able to persuade her otherwise – once she had decided on a course of action. His heart sank. She would just do it on her own if he did not help, and who knows what sort of trouble she could get into if he were not there?

She had always had a mom growing up, and although that made her more independent and confident, there were still areas where she really could do with some male insights at times.

"Well…." He agreed reluctantly, "I suppose we could try."

"Great! Let's have a look at that paper again."

He handed her the paper. "Perhaps we should protect it. You know, like they do on TV – put it in plastic."

"OK. But not until we've examined it first." She took out her magnifying glass. "Yes, it is not ordinary paper."

"I could have told you that without the magnifying glass," he grumbled.

"And then you would not be a proper detective. No, I wonder to whom we could speak in order to find out?"

He groaned. Her lapses into grammatical correctness were as humorous as they were irritating. "Go to a stationery store?" he suggested.

"No – they are not knowledgeable about all species of paper. What we need is someone who sells lots of different kinds of paper. Or a calligraphist – they are sure to know smart paper when they see it."

"What is a calligraphist, and how on earth do you know what they are?"

"My dear," Elizabeth wrinkled her nose at him, "there is such an invention as the internet." She smiled, and his heart bounced – for the second time that day. The first had been when she had greeted him in the early sunlight. "There are few calligraphists left – it's the art of fancy writing. Very beautiful – and almost dying because of computer fonts. But not quite."

"OK. But how do we get hold of one? And what if they want to charge us? And how do we pay for transport? Neither of us is exactly rolling in money."

She looked at him in pity. "Don't be such a wet blanket. Everything will work out – you'll see."

He sighed. It normally did – though how, he couldn't fathom.

"Let's go to the library, and to the internet!" She made it sound like an adventure, instead of the hard work that it would be. The problem was, he thought, she was just not realistic.

They popped the paper into a little piece of see-through plastic, and set off for the Alex library.

There they went onto the internet at one of the computers and discovered that there was a calligraphist in Sandton City. Germaine Van Tonder – in a shop called the Paper Stop. "Let's go!" Elizabeth squealed.

She always spoke in exclamation marks, Themba observed. So melodramatic. "How?" he responded. "We don't have the money to get there. What if she's not there? What if we ..." his voice trailed off with her interruption.

"Oh money! That's not important. We can walk." she said dismissively

He winced. It took an hour to walk to Sandton City from where they were. "We'd best start then....Oh!"

"What is it?" she queried.

"The man. I'd quite forgotten him." He looked at her crossly. "It's your fault."

She laughed. "So what do you want to do?"

"We'd better go and see that he is alright. I don't want him to die in our house!" He paused, then added, "I would also like to get my lazy older brother to look after him." Moses was good hearted, but very reluctant to do more than he absolutely had to.

"Alright. Then we'll pop by your house first." She hesitated. "We also have to decide where to leave the brooch. You never know when a *tsotsi* might try to mug us."

He considered momentarily. "My roof. I have a secret hidey-hole there which is invisible to the naked eye. You can't see it if you are not looking for it, and no one else will know that it is there."

"Agreed. Let's jog. I feel too excited to walk."

They entered his house quietly. The man was still breathing peacefully, and his wound did not seem to be bleeding any more. "What I 'm worried about is infection. So much could go wrong, especially if the wound is deep." Elizabeth spoke knowledgeably.

"It's all yours, Miss Nurse."

"No, I think we should ask your brother. He knows enough about wounds from his army days to attend him."

Themba grabbed a chair, and reached toward the ceiling beam. He touched a small knob and a little door swung open, revealing a small space. Taking the brooch from Elizabeth, he carefully wrapped it in a piece of tissue, then placed it gently in the hole. He clicked the wood back firmly into place, engaging the locking mechanism he had invented.

"Wow!" Elizabeth intoned. "I'm impressed."

Careful not to show how pleased he was, he jumped off the chair and went to waken his brother. It was amazing how soundly he slept – seen as they only had one room to live in. Others in the township were fortunate enough to have walls to divide sleeping from cooking – but so many of them had no such luxury. They were used to it, but it had its stresses.

Moses having sleepily agreed to see to their guest, they set off to Sandton. He did not know what would happen once his brother knew the full story, or realized what had just happened, but Themba was happy to leave that to a later date.

The lady in the Paper Stop was very happy to assist – especially when Elizabeth explained to her that is was part of a mystery they were trying to solve. Her kindly face twinkled up at them from the counter. "Oh my dears," she breathed excitedly, "How wonderful!" She glanced at the paper. "Hmm...it's linen paper."

Elizabeth glanced excitedly at her partner in crime. "You see!" she cried. "I knew we should have come. Who would have known about linen paper?" She turned to the calligrapher. "Where was it made?"

"Hard to tell. It's certainly not made in South Africa – the paper that we use for art canvases is similar, but this is fine paper – enabling it to be used for writing. No – it must be made in either The United States or Ireland. My guess is that it is more likely to be Ireland, seen as writing paper in the US is more likely to be used for printing than writing. It's possible that the owner of this paper had a monogram stencilled on the top, and that they had to bulk order somewhere. Now...." The lady paused to look more closely at the paper. "It normally has a watermark to signal its quality. I think I can see part of one here, and I will see if I can find out where it was made." She looked up. "Do you think you could leave this here?"

"No, we...." began Elizabeth, but Themba interrupted her.

"Yes," he said firmly. "Of course we can. How long do you think you'll need?" Ignoring Elizabeth's glare, he continued. "If you can just keep it in the plastic as much as possible – you never know when we may need it."

"Of course," the lady breathed. "And I'll wear gloves to protect it from fingerprints."

Looking at his partner's chagrined face, Themba intoned quietly, "Thank you. We would value that." He added, after a moment's deep thought, "Perhaps we could just copy down the words."

Germaine smiled and complied, copying it very carefully onto a scrap of paper.

"It was the only thing we could do," he explained as they walked back to Alex. "If we had not left it there, she would not have been able to trace the paper – bar taking a photo, which is exactly what we don't want. Evidence like that should not be copied. It could get dangerous. "

"You're right," she acknowledged, tilting her head at him.

"At least I get something right," Themba grumbled.

"Nonsense!" she laughed. "Yours is a sound and steady head where mine has got midgets. Without you I would find myself quite stranded a lot of the time. You are so steady. And Right so much of the time."

Gratified, Themba subsided into a contented silence while Elizabeth continued to chatter. "We've still got that writing to decipher. I do wonder what it means. What language it is. One thing for certain, it's not an African language. You can tell somehow. It seems European or something."

Themba smiled wryly at the language-expert-in-the-making. There wasn't anything Elizabeth wouldn't try to explore and experiment with - the fact was she was rather good at a lot of things. Her instincts never failed her.

"What we have to do next," she added, "is go back to your shack and question the man.

"If he can even answer us," he inserted, before she could say anything more. "He is in a very weak and fragile state, and probably very confused. We're unlikely to get anything useful out of him."

"Oh, pyjamas!" she quipped. "We could always try."

"You're always inventing new uses for words," he complained. "Never know quite what you mean."

"Naturally." Her mischievous smile seemed to reflect onto the pavement. "One should never be predictable."

Themba looked at her sideways and muttered, "OK, we can try, but we must be careful…we don't want to push him too hard. Remember, we can't take him to a hospital."

"What do you take me for? A Nazi concentration camp guard?" she parried playfully. "Let's go!"

The Mysterious Stranger Speaks

The arms of the cool shadows hugged the co-conspirators as they opened the door to Themba's one-roomed house. The room had a mattress at one end, curtains (permanently drawn over the windows), a few cupboards and a *two-plate*[25] on a kitchen counter.

They slipped in softly and tiptoed over to the bed. The man was breathing peacefully – as was Moses.

"Much help he's been," whispered Themba, then turning to the man, he called softly, "Sir! Please wake."

The man opened one eye and wobbled his gaze haphazardly around the room. Finally, he found Themba's face. A look of confusion and bewilderment wrestled with the man's features for a moment, but it cleared as quickly as the striking of a match.

"Ah," he gasped, "the rescuer." A fleeting spasm of pain prevented him from speaking, but he took a few deep breaths and continued, "Thank you." His eyes rested on Elizabeth questioningly.

"Elizabeth", answered Themba, "and I'm Themba. "

"What's your name?" the words barrelled from Elizabeth's lips like little gunshots.

Themba frowned, but the man didn't seem too stressed by her impetuous outburst. "Sipho. Or at least that's what you can call me. It's a common enough name. I can't give you my real name. It'll be too dangerous for you if you know. The less I tell you, the less you will get into trouble."

Before Elizabeth could say anything, Themba stepped in firmly. "We want to know what you want us to do with you.

---

[25] *Twoplate*: Township-speak for electric stove, consisting only of two cooking plates.

You are badly wounded, and I am worried that you will die if we don't get you to hospital."

Sipho grimaced and nodded. He was a tough, strong man, so for him to acknowledge it might be life-threatening meant he must be in a great deal of pain. He muttered, "Piece of paper. Pen."

Themba went over to his school satchel. He picked up one of his well-thumbed iris-lined books, and scrabbled around for a pen.

"Hurry!" cried Elizabeth, "He's going!"

Themba rushed across the room. "Here! Quickly"

Elizabeth guided the pen and paper into the man's hands. Weakly, he printed a telephone number, holding the pen with two hands in the effort. He reached to his top pocket for his mobile phone, but couldn't grasp it.

"Here, let me help you," suggested Elizabeth. She whipped the phone out, but Sipho's head had fallen back on the pillows.

"I think he wanted us to use it to phone this number," Themba declared. "Let's hope it's a doctor."

Elizabeth was already tapping in the number. "Hello, "she almost shouted, "Are you a doctor?"

The voice at the other end of the line spoke: "I am certainly connected with the medical profession," it said wryly. "I recognize this number. Who are you?"

"Oh, we can't waste time with introductions," cried Elizabeth breathlessly, "This man has been severely wounded and must get to a hospital immediately. I think…. I think he is dying."

Without further ado, the man asked for their directions, and put down the phone.

"What now?" asked a bewildered Elizabeth. "What is going to happen?"

"I guess we wait," replied Themba.

It was not long before they heard a soft knock at the door.

"Wait," whispered Elizabeth as Themba walked toward it. How do you know it won't be the *tsotsis*?"

Themba smiled and walked to the door.

"Themba! Stop!"

"They will let us know that we phoned them – that's how we'll know they are the right people."

Sure enough, as they opened the door, the men mentioned the call. "This is the number you phoned," one of them added for reassurance.

"Quickly!" Elizabeth pulled them in and slammed the door. "Here, on the mattress."

She saw that the men had a stretcher-like contraption with them. They brought out a suitcase...she could have sworn that they had not had it at the door. How had they contrived to make it appear?

Rapidly, they put Sipho on a drip, rebandaged the wound, and placed him very gently on the stretcher.

One of the men spoke into a walkie-talkie. "Ready," he uttered tersely.

They heard the sound of a fight break out a little way down the road, then a screech of brakes, and the door burst open.

"Diversion tactics," explained the man when he saw the look of bewilderment on their faces. They lifted Sipho out of the house and into the car waiting at the door. How they had got there was a story in itself, as that section was inaccessible to cars. Elizabeth and Themba looked out at the crowd gathered round the people down the road. The scenario looked very real....with loud shouting, and even a few punches being thrown around. No one was looking their way.

They bundled him into the 4x4, then raced off.

"Well! Of all the exits! What if we want to contact them?" complained Elizabeth. "You never know, we might need to ask them questions. Or tell them something."

"We have that phone number," Themba reminded her. "We can contact them on that."

"If it remains in use," remarked Elizabeth bitterly. "Oh well, at least we have our clues. We can start with the brooch again.

She paused, "Hey! Sipho left that behind! How on earth are we going to get it to him?" She stopped, then grinned. "Well, we have the clue now. We can give it back later. But which jeweller would know about this kind of brooch?" she mused. Themba watched as different ideas flitted across her face. She was so see-through – like a diamond sparkling in the sunlight.

"I know!" he said, "Let's just work our way from jeweller to jeweller – starting at Alex Mall."

"That'll take a lot of work."

"Well you wanted to be a detective."

"Fair enough," Elizabeth admitted. They retrieved the jewel from its hiding place. "Now, let's go on the march." She linked her arm through his and smiled up at him. "What ho Watson!"

Sandton

The first jeweller could not help, so they decided to continue the next day, as it was rather late, and they were pretty exhausted from all the traipsing around. Naturally, they did not want to be out of the house after 7pm – as far as was possible.

The following day, they took a taxi to Sandton.

"We can't walk twice in one day" commented Elizabeth, "And I told you we had some money."

"Where did you get it from?" Themba asked suspiciously.

"What you don't know can't harm you," smiled Elizabeth mischievously.

"Elizabeth, what have you done now?"

"Nothing illegal, don't you worry."

The glint in her eyes suggested something naughty, but he wasn't about to ask.

The truth was that she had sold some goods that she had been donated, and she was feeling rather flush. She didn't want Themba to know it was her own money, or he might refuse to use it.

The first set of jewellers could not help them. They hadn't even known where to begin.

"Never mind," said Elizabeth, "We'll walk till we find one."

It turned out to be an optimistic statement. They trudged through twenty-three stores throughout the city before they got a positive response. 'Solomon's' was a little room tucked away in an obscure alleyway of Sandton. It had not looked very promising on the outside. It had seemed a rather old fashioned – nothing to suggest an upmarket jeweller or any form of wealth. It had a rather dingy interior, with a worn mustard carpet and tired–looking yellow walls. The room also had a musty odour, as well as a faint aroma of spice.

The jewellery cabinets displayed few items, so the two young detectives were about to turn away when an old man called out to them from the back of the shop with a thin, hoarse voice, "What do you want?"

Ever polite, the two stopped for a moment. "Well," began Themba, "We were really looking for someone who can tell us about a very special piece of jewellery." He proffered the brooch as the man shuffled forward.

"Ah", muttered the old man, who was presumably Solomon, "Yes, this is a very good piece of jewellery. Most beautiful. Most beautiful." He repeated. He pondered some moments, and then quavered, "This is representative of the work of Elzette. A stick-pin, of pure gold and rubies."

Excitedly, Elizabeth nudged Themba. "You see!" she whispered.

"Elzette de Beauharnais," continued Solomon, "was a famous jewellery designer who made jewellery for top families in the world in the 1950s – especially for the world of the Spanish Mafia. The Mob."

"The Mob!" exclaimed Elizabeth impetuously. "No way!"

The man looked at her through narrowed eyelids. "How did you come by this jewellery?" His voice quivered with suspicion, and his eyelids flickered nervously.

"We…" began Elizabeth.

"My great aunt recently died and left it to me," interrupted Themba – once again. "She was very fond of me, and thought it might have a little bit of value. She had gotten it as a sort of pension-present from her employers. "

Elizabeth looked at him admiringly. He had come up with that excuse unusually quickly, and it was a very plausible story.

"Hmm." The man seemed more or less convinced.

"Who was it she said she worked for?"

"I don't know," said Themba with relief, glad to be able to fall back on the truth. "She had dementia for many years, and I did not think to ask her when she was well. Didn't really know much about life back then. Perhaps my parents would know," he added helpfully.

"Well….sure. It certainly is American Art Nouveau jewellery. This wave and the stone it contains is symbolic of something, but I would have to do a bit of research before I could tell you what it is. Perhaps you could let me keep the piece?"

"Yes," answered Elizabeth.

At the same time, Themba answered, "No! Thank you, but I would really not like to see this leave my sight."

"Very wise. Very wise." murmured the old man, replying to Themba and not Elizabeth. "Let me just take a photo of it." He took out his cell phone and carefully snapped a picture.

"Now, how do I get hold of you?"

"Perhaps we can come back in a few days' time. Will that give you enough time to investigate?" Themba spoke loudly and firmly.

"Yes," responded the old man slowly. "It certainly should be ok."

The two walked out of the shop. Themba looked lost in thought.

"I don't trust him," remarked Elizabeth. "I somehow feel that that stooped and rounded old man is wicked. "

"My sentiments exactly," answered Themba.

"I don't know how you came up with that story so quickly," said Elizabeth.

"I thought that up whilst walking around looking for jewellers," he said. "I thought we might have to come up with an explanation for our possessing that br...uh.. stick-pin."

"How clever!" exclaimed Elizabeth. "I do think we make a good team." She smiled up at him, gave his arm an affectionate squeeze, and walked a little while in silence.

"What now?" she asked. "We don't quite know where to go from here? So far, all we have is Irish linen paper, a wounded man and a few more strangers, all of whom seem incredibly well organized. They were even capable of creating a distracting riot at short notice. "

"And then we have the stick-pin, which comes from America, and may or may not be connected to the Mob," added Themba.

"Don't forget the telephone number," said Elizabeth.

"The telephone number," he mused. He pursed his lips, looking intently at the ground.

"Yes?" whispered Elizabeth excitedly.

"Nothing. That is, nothing of great importance."

"Oh come on, there obviously something big on your mind."

Themba just shook his head and lapsed into silence. He was considering glumly that they weren't great detectives. They had done a lot of traipsing around, and found out one or two details, but they had not reached any conclusions.

"Wait" shouted Elizabeth. "We've forgotten one thing....the writing. We need to find out what the writing says, and what it means."

Themba's face brightened. There was still one clue to investigate. Perhaps it would lead them a little further forward, and they would start making headway in this case.

The Super Sleuths

The interior of the shack was cool…unlike most shacks, it had a good through–draft of air, and had a tree overhanging the roof, so that when the sun shone fiercely, it did not heat up and sear the room underneath. The walls were white - painted straight over the brick, and they had actually managed to put in two windows – front and back, although, like all of Alex, the curtains were permanently closed to fiercely nosy neighbours.

They found Moses up and about, listening to Angie Ntuli's most popular music. Themba did not like it, but since it had been all the rage for many years, he had not choice but to listen.

"Where have you two musketeers been?" Moses queried. Moses was a film-boff, and knew just about any character in any film that had been made since 1960. Where he got the time to watch, Themba did not know.

They recounted their adventures to him. At the end of their recital, he gave a wry grin. "Quite the detectives, aren't you? Move over Hercule Poirot, here come the Teenage Sleuths."

"Teenage Sleuths!!" Elizabeth clapped her hands. She turned to Themba. "Let's call ourselves that."

"Fine by me," he said, "but what if this case lasts beyond next month, when we both turn twenty?"

Crestfallen, Elizabeth remarked," True…well, perhaps we can call ourselves the Super Sleuths then."

"Sure," Themba said uncomfortably, "but don't you think we'd better leave the real detective work to the police? "

"Nonsense!" exclaimed Elizabeth. "There are a million things we can do - look at all those clues we have followed up already. Besides which, how can we go to the police with what we have? They would just laugh at us. A wounded man. A scrappy message and a stick pin. Apart from the man who was shot, and who is no longer here, we have nothing for them to take up – no leads. "

Moses said, "Seems like you're beaten *buti*.[26] You can always take your findings to the police once you've found out a bit more."

"Ok," agreed Themba a little reluctantly. Then he added in a more upbeat manner, "It *is* rather exciting, isn't it? We are having quite a lot of fun, and I am very motivated to get to the bottom of this. Whatever *this* is." Then he added a caution, "we just need to make sure we go to the police as soon as it gets dangerous."

"Done!" said Elizabeth. "As soon as there's the faintest whiff of danger, we'll tell the police."

"I think there's already been enough danger," grumbled Themba. "You were not the one who had to hide from those gunmen," he pointed out, "and there was something about that Solomon-person. "

"True," commented Elizabeth dismissively, "But we're fine. No harm came to us, did it?"

Moses turned to begin cooking supper. He was an excellent cook, and enjoyed surprising his small family with dishes from around the world. He brought out a big pot to cook the pasta in, and went outside to fill it with water. The tap was a communal one for several shacks in the shared courtyard. They heard him start to fill the container, and then they heard his voice shouting at someone in a friendly way.

"He'll be a while," said Themba. "Let's look at that paper."

He took the scrap of paper out of his pocket, and examined it.

"Well, I certainly can't make much sense of it. I can't think of anyone whom I could ask either." Elizabeth sounded doubtful, for once.

"It's just possible that I may know someone," announced Themba rather secretively.

"What! You've been keeping secrets!" said Elizabeth, playfully accusing.

---

[26] *Buti*: brother

"She's an old school teacher of mine. She used to teach at St Mary's, where I took extra lessons last year."

"Right, let's find her then!" said Elizabeth, starting up.

"You forget how late it is," remarked Themba, folding the paper. "I think it's best not to go out right now. You know full well how dangerous Alex can be after 7 at night."

Just then, Moses walked in with a couple of men. They were thick-set, and looked like bouncers from the local *shebeen*. They wore black shirts, black jeans, and large gold chains round their necks. "These men were just asking if we had seen anyone unusual around yesterday," he said. "I said that we hadn't, but they insisted on asking you themselves."

He motioned to the two sleuths, who were standing frozen at the back of the shack. Slowly, so as not to draw attention to the movement, Themba picked up a dishtowel to cover the paper. Hopefully, they would not have seen him holding the paper as they arrived. Not that they would know what it was, but still, he felt the need to hide it, somehow.

His head thudding from the beating of his heart, he shook his head. "There are always strangers around Alex," he said truthfully. "Yesterday, I saw two white people go into a shack just two doors…"

One of the men interrupted him. "No, no, it's a black man we want. Probably wounded. Well built. About mid- thirties."

Themba shook his head. The men were not to know that it meant, "No, I'm not going to tell you," rather than "No, I haven't seen him.' He added, "We'll certainly let you know if we see him." He hoped they wouldn't notice he hadn't answered the question. Then, with an innocent air, he asked, "How do we get hold of you?" With added bravery, he asked, "Can we tell him what it's about?"

The men frowned at him. They were certainly not in the mood for answering questions, but one of them must have thought better of it, and with a brighter air, said, "He won a lot of money at the casino last night, but left it behind when someone tried to fight him for the money."

They certainly rivalled him in inventiveness, he thought.

"You can get hold of us on this number." One of the men stretched out his hand. Elizabeth saw with excitement that it was a business card, with a swirl on it that reminded her of something. Swiftly concealing her emotion, she nodded dumbly at them.

Themba looked at her in surprise, but then bowed his head, and waited for the men to leave.

"Oh!' she squealed after the prerequisite silence they had waited when the men left. "Now we have a further clue! Hooray!"

They looked at the card. It was glossy, and looked expensive. It was black, with red embellishments. The heading was *Jimmy's Saloon*, based in Thembisa. "Aha! No wonder - Thembisa," Elizabeth said, with the popular Alex-disdain for the place. "So many criminals there."

Themba laughed. He felt sure that the people from Thembisa said exactly the same thing about Alex.

"Oh look, there is a big swirl here in the corner of the card. Under the clenched fist." Elizabeth's voice rose. "I remember seeing it somewhere." She paused. "Now where was it?" Her voice faded away as she thought back through the day.

"Musa Ndoga. Controller. Call..." Themba read aloud. "Well, perhaps we can find out a bit more about them from our Thembisa friends. "

"Well, since we have a few leads to follow, why don't we split the tasks? You can go and see your teacher, and I can go to Thembisa."

"Thembisa will be dangerous. If those *tsotsis* find out you have been asking questions about them..." Themba drew his forefinger across his throat.

"You're right. Well, then, we'll go together." She twirled around on her right leg. "I'm going to be a world-famous detective!!"

Themba laughed, and corrected, "We," he said. "*We* are going to be world-famous detectives."

"We," murmured Elizabeth softly. "World famous." She smiled at the door, and left for home.

Miss Jelly

Themba's teacher was called Miss Jelly. She had a rounded figure, and her face with its rosy cheeks seemed lit by laughter, even when she wasn't smiling.

She glanced at the paper. "Spanish," she declared, hardly even examining it. "I don't know the language myself, but I have a friend who is fluent. Shall I call her?"

Themba and Elizabeth smiled their acceptance, and Miss Jelly turned away to find her mobile phone. Really, Themba thought, Miss Jelly was like a pair of old shoes – comfortable and familiar; always bringing a sense of stability and purpose. She always seemed to have solutions for questions, even if she had to refer to others to get it. In that way, Elizabeth was a lot like her.

"How interesting!" they heard her exclaim. "That simply makes it all the more puzzling." She turned back to them. "It..." She paused sniffing the paper. "Roses. Antique Rose. The smell that only DKJ makes."

Themba looked at her- he had forgotten to ask Elizabeth, and had only now been reminded of his intended question.

"Yes," confirmed Elizabeth, passing her nose over the paper, "Only DKJ makes this exclusive Rose smell. Quite a distinctive perfume, and something that few could afford."

His eyes responded with a question.

She smiled. "We who can't afford any perfume – never mind this expensive brand – go to the shops to try out the 'test' perfumes. And when we go out somewhere special, we go into a store to put on our favourite perfume as though we are 'testing' when we are on our way to the venue. That way, even the poor can smell nice."

He frowned. He wasn't sure how ethical it was, exactly, but he supposed if shop owners put out perfumes for trial, that there could be no objection if a spritz was used not for 'test', but for 'wear' purposes.

"So that's how you know your perfumes!" he murmured.

"Yes!" she smiled. "I'm very good at it too."

He grinned. "No prerequisite for modesty, I see."

"Not if you're going to be me," Elizabeth answered with a laugh.

She turned to Miss Jelly. "Now, as to the meaning of those words...."

"Well, all they mean is this: 'You will find it in the house of the terrorist (or freedom fighter) NM – garden – beneath the pepper...' There it stops. There is no explanation of whether it is a pepper tree or a pepper plant."

"Didn't know there was a difference," uttered Elizabeth.

"NM! Of course! Nelson Mandela." Themba felt proud of himself – for once he had been mentally quicker than Elizabeth. "Nelson Mandela used to live on 7th Avenue," he added unnecessarily.

She looked at him kindly – she was not going to tell him that she had guessed the great Madiba as soon as she had seen the paper. He would feel so chagrined. No, it was better to leave him to enjoy his moment of triumph.

"The pepper tree has absolutely nothing to do with the peppers that we eat, does it?" queried Themba.

Miss Jelly replied, "No, but this piece of paper would have been able to distinguish the difference between pepper tree and pepper plant if we had had just one more letter of the writing. Male or female endings would give us a complete answer." She paused. "Of course, if it had been a pepper plant, it would have been dug up long ago. A pepper tree would be a safer bet."

Elizabeth and Themba scurried back home. After a hurried farewell to Miss Jelly, with a hearty hug from Elizabeth, they had decided to dash home. They wanted to visit the house on 7th Avenue straight away.

They wended their way through the cars and people – all shouting and hooting at each other. There seemed to be some sort of traffic jam up ahead, and some of the drivers had ramped up onto the pavement, trying to get around it. The goats and the people were in the street, attempting to squeeze past the minivans and cars. When they got closer, they saw that it was a definite gridlock – cars attempting to turn were blocking others, who in turn blocked those who needed to move for the first cars to move.

Themba and Elizabeth laughed. Shortly, someone would become an impromptu policeman and start bossing the traffic around. Many of the bystanders would join in, and their coordinated efforts would eventually lead to the unlocking of the puzzle. The drivers didn't mind - it was the only way to get out these messes. It normally came from everyone wanting to go their own way at the same time, and not giving way to others, but it only produced some mild irritability, and a great deal of enjoyment from bystanders.

They found they were in front of the open-air butcher, with the flies buzzing round the meat and the blood on the pavement. "Ugh!" exclaimed Elizabeth, "I will never enjoy that smell! I find it nauseating."

All of a sudden, Themba looked up. A man was watching him intently from inside one of the taxis. The sombreness of his expression, and the narrowing of his eyelids gave Themba an extremely uncomfortable feeling.

"Quick!" he whispered to Elizabeth, "Let's get out of here!"

The nice thing about Elizabeth was that she didn't question or argue at these junctures. She sprang into action and in no time at all, they had wended their way out of the traffic and back home to 12th Avenue. They'd go to 7th some other time.

Thembisa

The ride to Thembisa was uneventful, and their friends there had been most helpful. The insignia apparently belonged to one of the biggest shebeens in the Southern Hemisphere, run by the gangster Musa Ndoga. It was officially licensed, but much underhand activity went on there, according to their friends' sources.

The covert menace entailed little white packets of powder. Everyone knew – even the police.

"Why don't they do anything about it?" asked Elizabeth.

"I guess they are paid off," replied the one friend. "Not all policemen are fine, upstanding citizens."

"Or perhaps," added another friend, "they have been threatened, or their families threatened. It's rather difficult to stand up to such power if you are a mere policeman."

Themba nodded shrewdly. It made a lot of sense. How then could they outwit these crafty men? They would be super-alert to threats, and would have tentacles that stretched everywhere.

"Please don't tell anyone we asked about them," he begged. "All of us could be in danger."

Their friends agreed. They knew all too well what happened to people who crossed those thugs.

Having accomplished what they had come to do, Elizabeth and Themba decided to pop by the shebeen, just to see what it was like. Of course, their friends agreed to lead them there. It was a rather exciting mystery, after all.

"We're not going to go in," cautioned Themba unnecessarily, "just to…sort of… look."

One of their friends rolled their eyes, but Elizabeth smiled sympathetically. He could be a bit like a cat with her kittens at times, but he radiated such kindness that no one could take offence.

They sauntered past the shebeen very casually, pretending not to even look at the giant men standing at the entrance. Elizabeth caught sight of one of their faces, and quickly hid her head. "Themba!" she whispered fiercely. "Duck!"

He glanced at her in some bewilderment, then quickly flipped his head away from the shebeen as he recognised one of the men that had come to their house. "*Eish*," he murmured, sotto voce, "they probably wouldn't have recognized us, but if they had..." He shook his head sorrowfully. "I don't know if I could have thought of something to tell them. And they would certainly have been suspicious if we hadn't anything to say." He swallowed. "Should we not go to the police?"

"Yes!" agreed Elizabeth, "right after we have collected the info from Solomon's store in Sandton. But first: what have we decided about the wounded chappie - Sipho? Is he the goodie? Or the baddie?"

Here, their friends decided to leave them. They had been helpful, but, were rather bored, and eager to go and jive at their house.

"I think," uttered Themba sombrely, "that the man must have been somehow connected with the police. For one, he gave us a name. Not his own name, but a name nonetheless. He wouldn't have done that if he were a crook. A crook would have ignored any politenesses and refused to give any name. Secondly, he would probably have harmed or threatened us, or his friends would. And, thirdly, he gave us a false name. A name that we could call him whilst we were with him, but that he said was a false name. Only an undercover cop would have done that. Not a criminal. A criminal would simply have stuck with giving no name." Here he paused to chew a sliver of grass, his eyes gazing distantly at the thoughts in his head.

Elizabeth watched him, ideas flitting across his face like little reflections. She smiled up at him, contented, for once, to simply listen.

"What's more, those people who came to fetch him were ultra-organised. Quick. And they were respectful to us too. They seemed to be very proficient in the First Aid department. Now tell me what criminal is going to be that knowledgeable in the medical field?"

"Good point," Elizabeth piped up, "I don't know what *tsotsis* would do, but it would seem to me they wouldn't go round getting medical degrees and then getting into something that doesn't benefit them. I also think that the man that I spoke to sounded educated, sophisticated and a really good leader. Gentle, but strong. I don't know that the average thug would sound like that." She sighed. "Trouble is, we don't personally know any real *tsotsis*, so how would we know?"

"One thing I remember quite strongly is that Sipho did not want the police involved. That seems suspicious to me. On the other hand, perhaps he was investigating policemen. Or perhaps he was just being careful not to get ordinary policemen involved."

"Do you know what I think we should do?"

Themba watched her eyes sparkling with delight.

"I think we ought to call that old man – you know – the one we spoke to on the phone, and tell him what we know. Also ask him some questions," she added firmly. "After we have gone to collect our paper from Germaine and the information about our stick-pin from Solomon."

"Ok, but then we go to the police – especially if we are unsure where we stand."

"Ok," Elizabeth affirmed, "I certainly wouldn't want to meet up with the baddies again."

Danger

Themba and Elizabeth returned to Sandton the next day. It was a rather tiring walk this time – it was an unusually warm autumn day, and the sky was that crisp Prussian blue so typical of this time of the year. However, because of the cool wind, the walk was not so enervating.

They first went to retrieve their paper from Germaine's Paper Stop. Unfortunately, that turned out to be a dead end, as she could tell them nothing further about the insignia. The one thing she could tell them, however, was that someone in South Africa had ordered a set of such linen papers about 3 months ago. It was not much to go on, so they decided to press on and visit Solomon's.

He, in turn, claimed that he had much he could tell them. "Let me just finish my phone call," he grumbled, "and then I will see to you." He hobbled back to the recess at the rear of the shop.

They could hear him talking to someone, but could not discern what he was saying, apart from one or two words. "I'll go 'n get some doughnut and Coke," suggested Themba. "It might take a while – I saw a shop not far from here."

He took quite a while choosing which doughnut he would have (and which to buy for his brother) that it was twenty minutes before he returned. He returned to an empty shop. The only sign of any activity was a wooden chair lying overturned near the door. Near it, two parallel skid marks decorated the scruffy carpet.

Puzzled, he made charged outside and ran down the street. As he reached the corner nearest the shop, he saw someone in the sideroad being shoved into the boot of a black Mercedes 4x4 by two burly men. What he saw caused icy fingers to claw their way round his heart, squeezing hard. As the car had sped away, he had realised that the clothes the person had been wearing had reminded him of Elizabeth, and he dropped everything and ran. The street was not busy, and he managed to get the number plate. However, the car soon disappeared, so he walked back to the shop, crestfallen and dejected. He reached the scrambled remains of his doughnuts and Cokes, and threw them away.

Themba went back into the shop, but there was still no sign of life - not even in the back recess. He banged the counter in frustration. Where was Solomon? He really wanted to ask him about what had happened. He went to pick up the phone in order to call the police. It was high time they knew the story. He outlined the story of the kidnapping, and he was informed that they would be with him within 5 minutes. In the meantime, he was to wait outside the shop, in case any of the *tsotsis* returned.

As he put down the receiver, he noticed a sheet of white paper on the floor. Not knowing quite why, he picked it up. On the desk was a note written in a rather wavery hand: "Brooch pin belonged to Angie Ntuli...not to let anyone know – at any cost!! Retrieve parcel at NM 9 pm tonight." Angie Ntuli! Surely not the famous international singer?! His eyes widened at the thought. Yes, she was well known for her wild extravagances, and her ability to keep bad company, but could she really be connected to the thugs? She was very wealthy, but crime? It was hard to imagine.

Without further thought, he picked up the phone, whipped out the piece of paper with the telephone number of the doctor that the wounded man, Sipho, had given them, and dialled it. If the police were to be here, then it would be safe to chat to this man, even if he happened to be on the wrong side. The man listened to the summary of his discoveries, and said that he would meet them all at the police station. "You must be very worried about your friend," said the man. "We'll do everything we can to help you find her. Just let us do the work this time. You have done a sterling job – better even than the Intelligence Services."

"Marghm!" mumbled Themba, a bit embarrassed. "We still don't understand what it is all about, nor how it all fits together."

"Don't' worry. As you've figured it out, we will tell you a lot, though not all, of the story. Just let's find your friend first. Now, get out of that shop!"

The police arrived as Themba was leaving, and he explained that Intelligence were involved. He showed them the note, and described the raw facts of Elizabeth's kidnapping. At the end of the recital, he started quivering like a mild earthquake. The walls seemed to wobble precariously, and the floor to form waves.

"Quick!" a policeman called, seeing his face, "Get this man to the car immediately!" They trundled him into the car, and set off for the police station in Alex. They left a few policemen to comb the shop and look through its papers. Everything was to be closely documented and catalogued, and might be taken as evidence. Already one of the policemen had spotted stolen jewellery, so everything was to be judged as suspect until cleared.

None of the other happenings really registered with Themba. His mind was ferreting over Elizabeth and what might be happening. At the police station, he was caught up in the whirlwind of people near the desk, and did not see Elizabeth, as she barrelled in on him like a gust of wind. Shocked, he could only stare, mouth agape.

"Themba! It's me! Elizabeth!" Although she seemed to be shouting, he could only hear her dimly.

After frowning at her as though finding it difficult to see her, he threw his arms around her and gave her a hearty hug. "How on earth…?" he shouted.

Elizabeth grinned at him. "Now, did you really think I wouldn't find my way out of trouble?" she uttered mistily.

Themba smiled. She always did, of course. There was no denying that!

"Well, aren't you dying to know? Of course you are," she said before he could even take a breath. "These men…."

"I saw you get put into the boot," he exclaimed.

"Yes. Well, after that it was fairly simple. You know that all cars have a catch inside the boot to open the door? Well, I found it, and once we had slowed down for a robot,[27] I popped it, hopped out and ran into the traffic. They didn't dare follow me. And then I came straight to the police station." She sighed. "Very simple really. Wish I could make it more exciting."

---

[27] *Robot*: traffic light in South African terminology

"The police have got the numberplate, and have just told me that they followed the *skollie* to a house in Houghton," Themba filled her in. "It fits in with the slip of paper I found on the floor at Solomon's." He quickly outlined the details, and then paused. "I .. I don't really know what it means, but the name 'Angie Ntuli' seemed to spark one policeman's interest. He has been on the phone constantly since then."

Elizabeth turned to see the policeman, who was talking to a tall, distinguished looking man in a grey suit. The latter seemed quietly powerful – the kind of man that you would heed without thinking. He was nodding slowly and sombrely at the detective, but as soon as Elizabeth heard him speak, it triggered a memory. She looked at Themba. "Isn't that....?" Her voice trailed off as she saw him nodding.

"Yes," he replied. "It is the doctor we spoke to on the phone when we called for Sipho. I called him from Solomon's."

"Goodness, you were busy," she exclaimed, "It seems like you have solved everything!" She smiled at him. "Quite the clever Supersleuth!"

"Not quite," he reminded her. "We still need to know how it all fits together."

A policeman came up to them, calling them to follow him. Mystified, they walked behind him to a sleek black car. It had darkened windows, and once inside, they found it had back seat like a limousine – some of them facing backwards. There was the man in the grey suit inside, along with the chief of police. The doctor was obviously very important, as the chief of police was sitting very deferentially at his side.

"I'm Mr. Dube," said the doctor.

Themba and Elizabeth looked at each other in puzzlement. He was not a doctor then?

"We're going to take you somewhere, if you permit. There are people you need to meet. We'd like to ask you some further questions if you don't mind." The doctor's tones were calm, quiet, and well-modulated. He did not need to create noise to carry authority. He simply exuded it through every fibre of his upright being.

Themba and Elizabeth merely nodded at his words. To tell the truth, they felt a little awed. The ride was silent.

Themba and Elizabeth did not dare speak until spoken to, and the men were completely silent. Finally, they had the sensation of going through some gates, after which they came to a stop on some gravel.

The light was quite faded when they stepped out, and they could not see the surrounds through the darkness, but the house was a mansion by any standards. Although the porch lights were on, they were hustled very speedily into one of the rooms, so that they didn't have time to take stock of their surroundings. It was a large library, with books covering every wall. It was panelled, with carpet of the deepest pile and the most luxurious gold colour they had ever seen.

Once again, they did not have much time to take in the surroundings before they were ushered toward a leather couch, where they stared with round eyes at the people before them. There were several people standing near a large wooden desk, with Mr Dube seated luxuriously in his chair. One person they did recognise – Sipho. They smiled at him, and he gave them a wink and a wave.

"Now," said Mr Dube sombrely, "we'll begin. Elizabeth and Themba, won't you tell us your story?" He nodded at Themba to begin, and Themba outlined the entire story, Elizabeth interjecting often to add some details or comments.

"It was fortunate that you found that piece of paper," Mr Dube commented at last, nodding slightly at Themba. "You may not be aware, but there has been a big drug-smuggling gang operating from Thembisa for some time now, but we had no idea where it was based, nor who the leaders of the organisation were.

We had been putting the pieces of the puzzle together, identifying the chain command from the bottom up, when they discovered that Sipho was a police-spy, and so they set out to kill him. Our months of work was lost. That is, until you came in. We had not connected Solomon's, or the shebeen, nor did we know who was at the head of the gang until today – Angie Ntuli. We knew it was someone famous, someone who travelled a lot, but we would never have put two and two together without your investigations. In fact, without you, it would have taken another 5 - 10 years, and who knows what would have happened in that time."

He paused. Elizabeth thought that everything he did and said was imbued with dignity, but that pause was somehow the most elegant pause she had encountered.

"We had not known where their headquarters were, but even a cursory surveillance this afternoon revealed that it was indeed the gang's centre of command. Even as we speak, police are raiding both the shebeen and the Ntuli home."

As he finished the sentence, the phone rang, as if on cue. Mr Dube murmured a few words of quiet rebuke, then waved his hand in the air in a gesture of resignation. "Ms Ntuli escaped. They were not at the house when it was raided, and someone got word to them. Now, we back where we started." He looked at the far wall as though he was seeing through it. "In any case, we would have had not solid evidence against her or any of the others, so it might be just as..." His voice trailed away as he looked at Elizabeth's face.

"Ms Khosa, you have an idea."

She nodded. "Yes, sir. But may I have a minute to think?"

He acquiesced, and she stared at the piece of paper they had shown Mr Dube – the one that had fallen near to where Sipho had lain. Finally, she looked up.

"What date is it today?" she asked abruptly.

"The 20th," Sipho chirped.

Themba looked at him in surprise. It was the first time any of the other members of the group had spoken. It seemed like Mr Dube garnered to much respect for anyone to dare speak up. Sipho must have more status than many on the group to have been able to voice a word.

"Then I think we've got them!" she uttered. "Here... the words that are written in Spanish tell us where something was hidden – in the garden of Nelson Mandela. And here...."she motioned with her finger, "it mentions the date. And a time. They must be going to collect or dig up whatever is hidden under the pepper tree."

Mr Dube beckoned for the paper. "Hmm," his deep voice reverberated, "you have a point, young lady." He smiled, and Elizabeth thought it was the most kindly smile she had ever seen in a powerful person. He motioned to one of the men in the room. "Set up a task-force to trap them should they come to the house where Nelson Mandela used to stay. Whatever was buried there long ago is obviously very important to them at this time."

His mouth twitched at Elizabeth's half wistful, half crestfallen expression. "Normally,, we do not have civilians at these events, as they could get messy, but as you have done such a sterling job, would you like to be in on the catch?"

"Would we!" squealed Elizabeth. "Thank you sir!"

"Mind you," warned the doctor, "you will be kept at a very safe distance, so don't try anything unintelligent."

"You can count on us to do exactly as we're told sir," answered Themba soberly. "We know just how dangerous those men are."

Denouement

A watch was put in some of the houses overlooking the courtyard in the house in 7th Avenue. Themba and Elizabeth were neatly ensconced in a house which gave them full view of the pepper tree.

Now, they waited wordlessly, hearts pounding and eyes sparkling at being allowed to be part of such a venture.

7 pm came and went. 7.15pm. 7.30 pm. "African time!" grumbled one of the policemen. "Even the crooks operate on African time."

Just then, a few men arrived with a well-rounded Mama-figure. "Angie!" hissed Elizabeth, digging her elbow into Themba.

They moved toward the pepper tree, and dug up the box.

"Freeze!" came a voice from behind them. One of the gangsters whipped round and pulled off a shot at the direction of the voice, but the rest simply raised their hands in the air. Fortunately, the police had not shot back, as they had sufficient cover, so no lives were lost.

Some of the men looked extremely angry, but others looked scared.

Angie simply looked at them, clicking loudly in disgust. She turned a sour face to the policemen, and walked to the car.

"Just as well she didn't see us," said Themba. "I would not anyone to take revenge."

Sipho came in with another policeman. "What we discovered in the box will put them all away for life. They had a record of all the names of the founders of the organisation; its financial structures; and the aims and purposes of its existence. Angie is a businesswoman, first and last, so, with all her record-keeping and business plans, we have a mound of evidence which we can use against them." He smiled at them. "All thanks to you two, mostly. The nation will naturally be grateful. We are definitely going to give you a reward."

Themba grabbed Elizabeth's hand and squeezed. "What a day!" he said. "Certainly the best day I've ever had."

"Now we can definitely call ourselves the Super Sleuths," she answered. "Imagine all the problems we'll solve."

"Just keep away from the deep stuff," answered the policeman. "You were lucky this time around, but next time...." He drew his finger across his throat. "Those people were extremely dangerous. It is quite by chance you were not seriously hurt or killed." He shook his head. "Angie Ntuli. Who would have thought."

Elizabeth hadn't heeded him. "We'll put an ad in the newspaper with our money," she said, "and..."

Themba stopped her with a laugh. "First celebrate," he said. "Then plan. First, the reward. It's not often two orphans (one a half orphan) from a township achieve something so amazing."

Together, they marched off to claim their reward.

Book Review: Please would you leave a book review on Amazon or on Goodreads. I would be most helped by your review. Alternatively, you can leave a review on my website - details on the next page. You have no idea how 2 minutes of your writing can impact me and impact others – it is like gold!

Social Links

Website:
https://kess9316.wixsite.com/kareness

Facebook:
https://www.facebook.com/BookPocketRainbow

Instagram:
https://www.instagram.com/k_ess_author

Thank you.

Thank you for your purchase of this book.

If you wish to know of a reputable organisation working with orphans and vulnerable children, to whom you wish to donate, please do donate to :
Rays of Hope
Hyde Park
Account Holder: Rays of Hope
Account: 1972126903
Branch Code: 197205
Swift Code*: NED SZ AJJ
*for international deposits

I worked for them myself, so I know that they are a legitimate organisation. They can be checked by looking at their website and checking the PBO number.

Website: https://www.raysofhope.co.za

ABOUT THE AUTHOR

Karen Ess was an Occupational Therapist, and worked in Cape Town, South Africa, and London, UK.

She also studied theology at London School of Theology, and worked in the ministry with university students in the UK, Guatemala and South Africa.

She then worked with an organization called Rays of Hope, in the township of Alex, South Africa.

Her deep compassion has led her to write a book about the things she saw and heard, whilst disguising the stories, and thereby to invite others to assist these people, who suffer greatly and bravely.

www.ingramcontent.com/pod-product-compliance
Lightning Source LLC
Chambersburg PA
CBHW030355180626
46812CB00007B/2893